FALLING IN LOVE AT NIGHTINGALE FARM

A heartwarming, feel-good romance to fall in love with

EMMA BENNET

Joffe Books, London
www.joffebooks.com

First published in Great Britain in 2023

Cover art by The Brewster Project

ISBN: 978-1-80405-725-4

CHAPTER ONE

The tall figure of Mark Williams pulled a thick coat closer across his chest in an attempt to ward off the January early evening chill. It was beginning to get dark and he had to get back to the farmyard. A lot needed doing before he was done for the night and it would all be far harder without light. But he needed a couple of moments to himself first.

His grey eyes looked out over his family's farmland; though perhaps not huge by modern standards, it appeared vast to Mark when he contemplated the amount of work required to maintain it. The overgrown fields where hundreds of cows and sheep used to graze were now largely deserted and needed mowing. Soon the hedgerows around them would start growing like crazy again and would have to be cut back, and the woods shouldn't go much longer without coppicing. The row of tumbledown cottages lying neglected to his right made his heart sink.

The view was certainly beautiful, but he'd stopped being able to appreciate it. Now, it felt like a huge weight around his neck. He let out a sigh at the sheer enormity of having all this and more to care for and tend; a burden he'd taken on, but certainly hadn't chosen. He ran his calloused hand through his dark hair, long overdue a cut he felt, though unbeknownst to him any woman who glimpsed it saw a definite resemblance to Poldark. With spring coming there'd be even more to do about the place, and without being able to afford to hire a new farm manager, Mark and his father would be doing all the work themselves. Somehow.

He trudged back down the hill towards the yard. The red-brick farmhouse with smoke furling from its chimney looked homely and inviting if you ignored the many lost tiles from the roof. The yard itself had an air of abandonment about it, like it missed its busy past with herds of animals and noisy machinery traipsing through. The cow shed was in the best condition of the farm buildings as it was the only one used for anything other than the storage of winter feed and straw and the little machinery they had left. The fencing in the paddocks next to the yard could do with being replaced before it warmed up and the few animals remaining were moved out to graze in them.

He could make out his dad, John, in his battered old Barbour jacket, far too large for his diminished frame, shooing the chickens into their coop (which was looking more rickety by the day) — was he even further hunched over than usual, or was Mark imagining it? He knew his father was drained and exhausted, all his drive and spirit spent — the loss of his wife, Lynda, Mark's mother, almost three years before had aged him terribly, and it had been a long time before he'd been capable of anything to do with running the farm. He'd been alone in his grief after handing over control of the accounts to his sister, Sue, aimlessly wandering the hills with his dog, his days empty and void of purpose, only alive when his only child, Mark, was able to visit.

It took over two years for John to admit to Mark what a catastrophic mess the business was in, and that was only because things had become desperate. Mark knew how much the farm had meant to his mother. Her family had worked it for generations and, though Lynda moved away from the farm for many years to go to university, and had ended up marrying a 'city boy', a horticulture student she'd met in the student union at the beginning of her second year, her love for Nightingale Farm had never diminished, and the couple set up their family home close by. Many happy summer holidays were spent there as Mark grew up, and when his grandparents passed away and the farm was left to Lynda, she didn't hesitate to move herself and her husband there — she knew how to organise the accounts, and deal with the suppliers and buyers. Bill, the farm manager, who'd been with the family for years and knew the farm like the back of his hand, would care for the animals and crops with a couple of regular farmhands, and seasonal workers when needed. John would enjoy a semi-retirement, running the small market garden, which he hoped to extend and add a Pick Your Own field to. Their future was happy and secure.

Then, less than a year into living there, Lynda got sick. She hid it from John for as long as she could, joking that her tiredness was simply a sign of old age catching up with her. Finally, the truth came out, and their lives swiftly changed into a routine of dreadful hospital appointments and test results. When their farm manager decided it was time to retire and left, it seemed a trifling problem compared to what they were already facing.

Lynda died, and John grieved, yet the farm still needed running, and without someone who knew the business at the helm, it began to haemorrhage money. Most of the animals were the first thing to go — John could neither afford to feed them nor the manpower needed to care for them. Whatever machinery could be done without was next — even the milking equipment went, it wasn't worth keeping for the tiny number of cows left.

Worried about how his father was really coping, not quite placated by how John claimed to be "absolutely fine", Mark had decided to make an unannounced visit. He'd arrived to find an old plough being hauled away, his father standing by the door of the farmhouse looking unkempt and sadder than it seemed possible. He grasped a small bundle of cash in his right hand.

Mark's suspicions about the state of the farm's finances, which he'd tried to subtly quiz his father about previously, were immediately confirmed. He enveloped his dad in a hug and decided then and there that there was no way he was going to let his dad suffer alone.

Father and son talked long into the night and Mark packed up his belongings from his flat in Brighton the next day and moved into the farmhouse. He'd never regretted his decision for a moment, but there were times when the weight of what he'd taken on threatened to suffocate him.

* * *

As usual, it was late as Polly Pressman walked home from work. A seasoned Londoner, she kept her senses alert, and her keys in hand, as she marched swiftly by the glare of the streetlamps along Clapham Junction. Starting slightly as a motorbike roared past, she was distracted by a bleep from her mobile — another WhatsApp message from her sister, Julie, containing yet another photo of her two perfect children busy being perfect, along with a reminder that Polly "really must find time to visit Mum and Dad soon". Polly decided to do herself a favour and reply to it in the morning. Julie would be long asleep by now anyway.

Letting herself into the front door of her building, she picked up her post from the hallway table — the usual mixture of ads for insurance companies, credit card statements and takeaway leaflets, she imagined.

Polly entered her own flat and dumped the post and her keys on the kitchen counter before gratefully easing her aching feet out of the boots she'd stupidly worn, forgetting how much they hurt in the excitement of the extra couple of inches they added to her diminutive frame.

She headed into the bedroom to change out of her work clothes and tie her long blonde hair out of her face. Noticing her dark roots as she walked past the mirror on her wardrobe door, she sighed — she couldn't afford to have her hair done professionally like she used to, she'd just have to do her best with a home dye kit. Thank goodness for YouTube videos, which were the only reason her hair still looked as professionally styled as it did. She removed her make-up, ignoring the breakout of spots on her chin — she needed to be getting more fresh air and eating healthier she knew. She'd start tomorrow. Or maybe on Monday.

Going into the kitchen, she poured herself a large glass of white wine, and put some pasta on to boil. She took a moment to catch her breath and stare out of the large window, her favourite part of her home, taking in the city at night from five storeys up. Usually, that view was enough, enough to remind her why she was still in London, still working as hard as she was so that she could afford to continue living here, with not much else in her life. But it didn't hit the spot tonight. She remained in a New Year's slump, three weeks in. At least she had a drink with her best friend, Alice, at the weekend to look forward to. That never failed to perk her up.

She turned her attention to the pile of mail she'd brought in and was surprised to see very neat penmanship on one of the envelopes. How long had it been since she'd received a handwritten letter in the post? Opening it, she pulled out a single sheet of paper.

Dear Polly,

You won't remember me, but we met a few times when you were growing up, and I did some gardening for your family. Apologies for my rather old-fashioned form of communication, and for my posting this to your home. I bumped into your mother today, and she thought that your work helping struggling companies turn themselves around might mean you'd be able to help me with my business, which has been losing money for a while now. She suggested this might be the best way for me to get hold of you.

*If you think you're able to assist, could you give me a call
on the number below?*

*Many thanks and best wishes,
John Williams*

Oh no, was Polly's first thought. She knew her mum was
only trying to help — it was sweet that she'd given Polly's
address rather than her mobile number, presumably worried
John might call when she was in the middle of an important
meeting — and she believed she did have a vague recollection
of him from her childhood, but there was no way she could
help him. She'd have to call him to explain and be careful not
to give too much of her situation away, in case it got back to
her family. They'd only fret and worry, and Polly still wasn't
ready to deal with that yet, although she was all too aware
that she'd have to at some point. Why did being an adult
have to be so complicated?

* * *

Polly put off telephoning John for as long as she could the
next day, but eventually guilt got the better of her, and she
called the mobile number provided.

It rang for an age, and Polly was about to give up when
a man's voice said, "Hello?"

"Hi, this is Polly Pressman, I received your letter?"

The line crackled and hissed.

"Excuse me?"

"It's Polly Pressman," Polly repeated, loudly.

"Oh! Sorry, the reception's terrible in the fields. John
here. Thank you for getting in touch."

"No problem, it wasn't clear from your letter exactly
what your business was, but . . ."

"Sorry, you've gone again!" said John stoically. "Pop
down whenever you like to have a chat and a look round, it's

important you see the place. The address is on my letter, it's easy enough to find!"

"The thing is . . ." began Polly, but the line died.

Bum, thought Polly. She called John's number again, but it was unavailable. Her next option was texting, but that seemed a bit rude, especially as he was a friend of her mum's.

She looked at the address on the letter: Nightingale Farm? Cute name. A quick Google search found several Nightingale Farms, a couple in Kent, as John's business was, but nothing that stood out to her. No wonder they're struggling if they're not even properly showing up online, Polly couldn't help thinking.

Adding the postcode from the letter to her search led to Polly at least locating the farm on Google maps.

She needed to work later, but it would only take her a little over an hour to drive to this place and a change of scenery would do her the world of good — some time away from her problems was exactly what she needed. If she left now, she could speak to John in person, explain that she couldn't help professionally, but maybe offer him a few tips to set him in the right direction.

She'd be back in plenty of time, and there was no way her mum could complain about the way she'd treated her old acquaintance.

CHAPTER TWO

Polly tried to enjoy the drive to Kent and make the most of being out of the city for a few hours, but the constant drizzle and the nagging worry that her battered little Volvo, which she hardly ever used in London, sounded like it was on its last legs, made the journey stressful.

She felt a bit ridiculous dressed up in a suit and her favourite heels and with a full face of make-up on, but it was technically a work meeting, and she wanted to come across professionally in case John reported back to her mum. An embarrassing confession for a grown woman, but there you go.

Polly knew most of the route, she'd grown up near Hartfield which was about ten miles from Nightingale Farm, and her parents, as well as her sister and her family, still lived there. The Kent countryside was beautiful even in the depth of winter and in the rain, it would be spectacular in just a few short months.

Google maps led her once she got closer, but she almost missed the rather weather-worn sign, half-covered in foliage, which directed her down the track leading to Nightingale Farm.

The road was very potholed, and she crawled along, flinching every time her poor car dropped into a dip. Mud splattered everywhere, even reaching the windscreen, as the wheels spun furiously.

Finally, she reached a metal gate, with a shabby-looking farmyard on the other side. Tall weeds grew out of the many cracks in the ground. A pile of rusting machinery filled a corner, and one side was taken up with various buildings, which had all seen better days — most were missing at least part of their roof, and only the largest shed had a door. Various much repaired hen houses dotted the edges.

A large house covered in ivy and with smoke coming out of its wonky chimney was at the far end of the concrete expanse. Presumably, that was where she would find John. Deciding against driving into the yard, which she could see contained some lumps of what looked suspiciously like old animal poo, and was so bumpy it would undoubtedly cause even more damage to her ancient Volvo, Polly got out of the car. She hadn't thought this through, she realised — she'd not taken into account that she'd be visiting an actual farm with actual cow pats. She hadn't even considered bringing wellies, not that she even owned a pair come to think of it, but why hadn't she at least thought to remember an umbrella? She'd just have to get to the safety of the house as quickly as possible.

Polly struggled with the bolt of the heavy gate, but with a heave got it free, at which point she lost control of the gate itself as it swung out of her grip. She cursed as she was sprayed with yet more water. Dodging the brown mounds and numerous puddles, she ran across the farmyard as fast as she could in her — now ridiculous — heels. The sound of a dog barking from inside the house made her jump.

She'd made it three-quarters of the way when she heard an angry voice call, "Oi! What the hell do you think you're doing?"

Polly spun around too quickly to face the speaker, her right foot landed in a large, slimy pile of fresh sheep droppings. Her beautiful shoes! Her leg came out from under her, and she found herself suddenly on the ground on her back. Too shocked to say anything straight away, she looked up to see her aggressor marching over. He was tall and completely covered in waterproof overalls so it was hard to take in much more of him, apart from his extremely angry face. The door of the house had opened, and before she and the waterproofed giant could say anything else to one another, Polly found herself being helped up by another man, also tall, but frail-looking and much older with a thick, white halo of hair and beard surrounding his lined, weather-beaten countenance.

"Are you alright?" her rescuer asked, then, intently examining her face, he exclaimed, "You're Polly, I remember you from when you were tiny! I'm John. How good of you to drive down so quickly!"

Polly opened her mouth to speak but received a sudden lick on the nose from a dog who'd seemingly come to join in the party. Presumably, he'd been the one barking from the house.

"Get off her, Dylan, you're not helping!" said John, taking hold of the dog, which Polly could now see was a very endearing black and white collie, and moving it away from her.

"She left the gate wide open!" announced the angry man. "And she's blocked the track with her car."

"I'm sorry, I didn't think," muttered Polly. "And it's only been that way for a couple of minutes. If you'd explained the problem and asked *nicely*, I would have moved the car to somewhere more convenient and closed your precious gate."

"Hopefully you'd have done that before the animals got loose," the man replied, indicating to a handful of sheep who'd made their way from one of the sheds and were merrily heading towards the open gate.

"If you were so worried about it, you could have closed it again before having a go at me!" retorted Polly. She'd given up her afternoon to drive here because John had said he needed help; she was soaking wet, covered in sheep poo, her shoes were probably ruined, and now she was being shouted at. This certainly wasn't what she'd signed up for.

"Now, now you two," said John, in the manner of a parent calming a sibling quarrel, "Polly didn't mean to do any harm. You shut the gate, Mark, while I get Polly inside so she can dry off. We're not expecting anyone, so her car will be fine where it is for a bit. If we do have a visitor, they'll beep their horn and we'll get the car moved."

"Fine," muttered Mark as he stomped off to deal with the gate.

In the end, it was only actually Polly's pride which was injured, and she'd reached the point where her anger and indignation were rapidly being replaced with embarrassment: what an entrance to make! Mark must think she was a total idiot — of course, she knew she needed to leave gates as she found them in the country. She'd been so focused on getting through the rain as quickly as possible so she didn't arrive resembling a drowned rat, she hadn't thought.

Polly followed John into the old farmhouse. They walked through a sort of boot room, where Polly left her manure covered shoes and coat, and then into a warm kitchen with a flagstone floor. Large and traditional, it was quite basic with white-washed walls, and no dishwasher or microwave, but it was clean and tidy, with a big Belfast sink sunk into a long countertop with cupboards underneath that ran the length of one side of the room. Two windows above the sink looked out onto the farmyard and a third, much larger window on the opposite side of the room gave a view of the surrounding grey sky and rolling green hills. Polly had to stop so she could take it in. Her beloved cityscape from her kitchen had nothing on this.

A large, pine table, which had definitely seen better days, was in the centre of the room, and on the far wall, the source of the heat — and the smoke coming from the chimney — was revealed as an Aga. John pulled a rather worn, but very comfortable looking armchair over to the stove and sat Polly down in it before putting the kettle on to boil.

By the time John had washed his hands and found three mismatched mugs and some milk, the kettle was singing and he set about making drinks.

"There you go," he said, handing Polly a large cup of tea.

"Thank you," she replied. "I'm sorry about what happened outside."

"Don't worry about it," John said, waving away her concern.

"That chap seemed very cross."

"He's like that at the moment, nothing to do with you. Money worries have taken their toll on us both in different ways."

"Is he your business partner?"

"My son. We run this place together."

"Oh, right." Polly paused, getting her bearings before slipping into professional mode. "So tell me more about the business you need help with — what's its nature?" She reached to take a notepad and pen out of her bag.

"It's the farm," John explained, holding his hands out wide. "Or what's left of it anyway. It was a thriving enterprise years ago. But these things change. It hadn't been doing so well before my wife Lynda inherited it and, well, since she passed away . . . Mark and I have done our best, but . . ."

"I'm so sorry about your wife," Polly murmured. Her memory of Lynda was no better than her childhood recollections of John. "I've never dealt with a farm before . . ." she continued, seizing on a polite way to extract herself from getting involved with his problems. "I'm not sure I'm the woman for the job . . ."

John's face fell, but he quickly recovered. "Well, you're here now and it looks like the rain's stopped. Let me give you a bit of a tour once you've dried off a bit so you can get a feel for the place."

John was so lovely, and he'd lost his wife. Polly didn't have the heart to tell him that, as handy as the money would be if she took on the job, she knew nothing whatsoever about farming, and had no desire to see around his muddy fields and draughty barns. This wasn't even the type of thing she had any experience with. What she wanted was to go home, change into some clean clothes, and put this whole sorry experience behind her.

Instead, she found herself borrowing a pair of too-big wellies and a raincoat and following John and Dylan the dog back outside.

Thankfully Mark wasn't anywhere about, Polly was keen not to face him again.

John led Polly round the yard, dodging random chickens who wandered around clucking at nothing in particular. Even to her untrained eye, it looked horribly neglected. Some sheep milled around, Polly couldn't tell if they were the same ones who'd tried making a bid for freedom earlier. John shooed them back into a field — it was clear how they got out, the gate was barely hanging on, and had a huge gap underneath which someone seemed to have tried to repair with some fencing wire, but this was coming loose.

The fields Polly could see were very overgrown, except for one, which contained a small herd of beautiful cows. There was a large orchard full of bare apple, pear and plum trees, the ground a mush of fallen leaves and rotten fruit remains. Conversely, round the back of the house was a well-tended vegetable garden, which, even on this grey afternoon in January, was full of winter cabbages, leeks and parsnips.

Once they'd finished going around the land close to the yard, John disappeared into the shed used to house the farm's remaining working machines and reappeared in a cloud of black smoke on a noisy old quad bike. He came to a halt in front of Polly and handed her a helmet. "We'll need to take the quad if we're going to get around the whole farm this afternoon," he declared.

Polly's initial reaction was to decline as politely as possible and get to the safety of her Volvo pronto, but as she was about to make her excuses, Mark came round the corner. Polly saw him take in the sight before him, and raise his eyebrow.

She couldn't say precisely what it was, but there was something in his expression that Polly immediately read as him knowing she was going to wimp out of getting on the bike. And that her doing so was proving he'd been right about his first impressions of her.

"Thank you, John," Polly said, accepting the helmet and forcing a large smile on her face. "Let's get going."

The look of astonishment on Mark's face took away a decent chunk of Polly's fear as the quad careered out of the farm yard and towards the hilly pastures in the distance.

* * *

The sun had almost finished setting when Polly and John returned to the farmyard a couple of hours later, unscathed if a little windswept. Polly took a surreptitious glance at her watch; she'd have to leave soon if she was going to get back to London in time for the start of her shift. She didn't relish the thought. A couple of hours of being out in the fresh countryside air had done her the world of good she was sure, and however hard their money troubles were, she couldn't help envying John and Mark living where they did. She felt calmer than she had in months, and the anxious knot in her stomach loosened as her nose turned red in the cold.

"The farm's about 350 acres in total, but we don't work all of it anymore," John explained as they hung their helmets up in the shed. "We did get some boys in to harvest the hay last year, but it's just been Mark and me for a while now. We can't afford regular help at the moment. We sold off most of the animals, and any non-essential machinery."

"So what do you make your income from?" Polly asked.

"The hay made a bit," John replied, "And I sell my veg, eggs, and some apples at the local market on a Thursday. I do well from that, but it's not enough. Thankfully the house and land were all paid off when my wife inherited them, but it still takes a lot to run a place like this."

"I bet," Polly said, as she scribbled down notes. After the last couple of hours, she couldn't help but be interested in this place and wanted to find out more about it. Underneath the neglect, she could see it was lovely, and there was so much potential.

If she'd been dealing with the farm through Streamline, she knew exactly what she would have been instructed to do: bulldoze the cottages and then divide the land up into neat little parcels to sell to developers if there was any chance of getting planning permission. If the council refused planning permission, sell the lot off cheaply. But she really doubted that was the route John would want to take. Or that she'd be able to follow through with those instructions.

Polly's mobile rang.

"Excuse me a second, sorry I need to take this," she said to John, seeing the caller was her boss.

"Hello," she answered.

"Hi Polly, Greg here. We won't need you for your shift tonight after all. Bit of a mix up with Tony."

"Oh, okay," replied Polly, keeping her tone light to hide her frustration. She needed the money from the extra shift, her car insurance was due in a couple of weeks.

"Should be more hours available next week though when Lucy's away," Greg said, in compensation.

"Pop me down for whatever's free," Polly said, checking over her shoulder that John wasn't listening in and that she wasn't saying anything too incriminating.

"Will do," Greg replied, and the call ended.

"Sorry," said Polly, turning her attention back to John.

"No problem. I think that's the tour completed anyway," said John. "Especially as it looks like it's going to start pouring down again any moment."

They walked back to the farmhouse in companionable silence, Polly's brain going nineteen to the dozen with ideas for the business.

She was pulled away from her thoughts by John asking, "Can you stay for supper? I've had a casserole in the Aga all afternoon, it's my wife Lynda's recipe."

"I'd love to stay," said Polly automatically. John seemed lonely, and what did she have to get back for anyway? An evening by herself in her flat, she could do that anytime, and she'd noticed how good the cooking smelt when she'd been in the house earlier.

"You make the cups of tea then," John said, "I'll get the veg on. I've got fresh kale picked today from the garden and potatoes."

"Great," said Polly, putting the kettle on. "How do you take your tea?"

"Milk, two sugars please, and Mark has his with just a splash of milk."

Polly's good mood went down a substantial notch: in all the fun she'd been having, she'd forgotten about Scary Mark. The last thing she fancied doing was having supper with him, but she'd already agreed, and it would be rude to back out now.

John put the potatoes on to boil. "I'll go and give Mark a shout," he said. "Back in a minute."

He went out into the yard, and Polly fiddled around preparing the drinks, enjoying the novelty of using a stovetop kettle, and then settled down into the old armchair next to the Aga with Dylan by her feet, looking out of the window over the fields.

Heat radiating from the Aga made the room feel warm and homely. She felt her whole body relax, and her eyes close.

"Quite comfy there are you?"

Polly's eyes shot back open. Mark was in front of her, an amused look on his face as he stared down at her. She couldn't help noticing he was a lot more handsome when he wasn't covered in waterproofs and shouting at her.

Embarrassed, Polly shot to her feet but she was saved from having to respond to Mark's comment by John arriving back.

"Have you two made up now?" John asked.

Mark and Polly scowled at one another but were both silent. John glanced between the pair and seemed to decide it best to leave the topic.

"I'll have a quick shower if there's time," said Mark.

"Plenty of time," replied John easily.

Polly felt herself relax once more as soon as Mark left the room again. That man really did have a terrible effect on her. He made her feel on edge and like he was watching and judging her.

She helped John lay the table and finish off cooking. Mark reappeared as they were serving up and took his place at the table. Polly had to walk past him to get to hers. As she did so, the smell of shampoo and, she supposed, Mark, hit her nostrils. Her mind couldn't help giving an involuntary jolt. He may be annoying and rude, but she couldn't deny that he smelled good. Very good actually. She felt herself blush and hoped that neither of her dinner companions noticed.

"This is delicious," she said to John. She hadn't realised how hungry she was, and the casserole full of tender beef, sweet onions and swede, seemed the perfect food to accompany the miserable weather outside.

John passed her over the basket of thick hunks of brown bread, spread generously with salty butter. "Thank you. Lynda used to make it a lot. She was an excellent cook."

"You must both miss her terribly," said Polly.

There was no response from Mark, who continued to look down at his plate, but John didn't seem to mind her comment, "We do," he said simply, before changing the subject. "So, tell us more about this company you work for . . . Your mother said you help struggling businesses by working out how they can make savings, and sorting out loans for them?"

Oh yikes, thought Polly. She'd been enjoying herself with John so much, she'd let go of her charade, and stayed longer than she should if she'd wanted to keep up her pretence.

"Um, yes," she murmured, frantically trying out different versions of how she should respond in her head in case anything she said gave the game away and got back to her mother, "That's exactly what they do, they're one of the top in the country in their sector. Did you bake this bread yourself? It's wonderful."

Thankfully, John took the bait and began to tell her all about the local bakery that delivered to them.

Polly felt uncomfortable, she didn't want to deceive or lead John on at all but didn't know what she could say to get around that. She ate as quickly as she politely could. As soon as she'd finished, she put her knife and fork together and said, "Thank you so much, but it's getting late, and I must be going."

"Oh, what a shame," said John.

"It's been so nice," said Polly, guiltily, "I loved seeing round, but I'm afraid I really can't help you. As I said before, farms really aren't my specialty, I usually deal more with restaurants and bars, clothes shops, that kind of thing . . ."

John's shoulder slumped and he seemed to deflate. He'd obviously expected the tour to have changed Polly's mind, or at least to have weakened her resolve. "Well, thank you for coming down anyway. It was nice to see you again after all these years."

"I really hope you manage to turn the farm's fortunes around and keep hold of it."

"Me too," John replied, sadly.

He went to get up, but Polly said, "Please, don't worry about seeing me out, enjoy the rest of your meal!" She slipped on her heels and was out of the door before John could put forward any objection. As she was closing the front door behind her, she heard Mark call out, "Don't forget to shut the gate!"

"Idiot," Polly muttered under her breath. She hurried across the farmyard as quickly as she could using the torch on her mobile to help avoid the worst of the puddles and the animal droppings. She possibly gave the gate slightly more of a bang as she closed it than the action warranted.

Driving away in her mud-covered car, Polly felt unhappy her afternoon had had to end as abruptly as it did, but she shouldn't have allowed herself to be charmed by John and the farm — there was no way she could help him, and she could very easily have given away the fact that she hadn't worked for Streamline for weeks. The problem with working for a consultancy company specialising in stripping itself down to ensure maximised profits so it was seen as an example of how the businesses it was paid to help should run, was that if they decided you weren't entirely essential to its running, you were given the boot pretty swiftly from a contract containing many, many clauses to protect the company, and leave the newly ex-employee with as little redundancy pay as possible.

So far Polly was just about covering her bills with the bar work she'd managed to find at The Bluebell, a dingy, old man's watering hole located off Balham High Street, although fewer shifts were available now than in busier periods. She needed to find some extra income soon.

* * *

Polly's shift the following evening was quiet. The usual regulars were in, nursing their pints and packets of pork scratchings, and a television in the corner played the football highlights.

She was going through her regular routine of obsessively wiping down the wooden bar which seemed to ooze stickiness from its very core, when she looked up to see her best friend, Alice, come in the door.

"Hey you!" she said, gingerly leaning over the bar to give her friend a hug.

Polly and Alice met on their first day at university and had been mates ever since, both choosing to stay in London after they'd finished their degrees. They looked alike, and people often mistook them for sisters, indeed far more so than when Polly was out with her actual sister, Julie.

"Can I get a double gin and tonic, sweetie?" Alice asked, handing Polly a ten-pound note.

"Rough day at work?"

"Yeah, two couples didn't even bother turning up for their viewings, and that crazy woman with the cats I told you about, is still refusing to accept that her house is overpriced and stinks of cat pee, and that's why it hasn't had a single offer in the six months it's been on the market." She shook her head, sighing.

Alice worked as an estate agent, a job she didn't exactly love, especially as it often involved being in the office on Saturdays, but which had meant her getting the heads up when the perfect little home for her and her boyfriend, Richard, came up for sale. Polly was in the position where she didn't see how she'd ever be able to get on the property ladder herself, but, right now, that was the least of her worries.

"Sounds like I should make it a triple," replied Polly.

"Sorry," said Alice, looking guiltily at her friend preparing her drink, "I shouldn't be complaining . . ."

"Don't worry about it," Polly said quickly.

"How are things going with you?" Alice asked. "Any job leads?"

"No . . . but I did have a strange afternoon yesterday," said Polly, and proceeded to fill her friend in on what had gone on the day before at Nightingale Farm.

"So this guy, John, and his son: they don't know you lost your job?"

"Nope."

"Well, why not help them out?"

"Because that would be dishonest, and because I know absolutely nothing about running a farm."

"Okay, firstly," countered Alice, "It is a tiny bit dishonest, but you're just doing freelance, independent work — and I'm sure they'd be getting you for a cheaper rate than going through Streamline. How about you say you'll only charge them if the farm starts making a profit again? If the stuff you suggest doesn't help, they won't owe you anything. Secondly, you can do some research and learn about farming I'm sure, and the way you're talking about that place, I bet you've already got some ideas up your sleeve. Thirdly, you're really, really good at this sort of stuff, regardless of knowing nothing about farms. Oh, and fourthly: you've got nothing better to do with your time, let's face it."

"That last one was a bit mean . . . but true," said Polly. "You are right, I do have some ideas. To be honest, I haven't been able to stop thinking about the place since I left. There's so much potential there, but I think they need to play to their strengths . . ."

"It's them you should be telling, not me," said Alice, with a smile.

"Your idea of only charging them if things work out is good, though I'd still feel guilty lying to them . . . but I can't tell John the truth until I've confessed to Mum and Dad that I got made redundant."

"Well, I've told you my opinion about that," Alice said firmly. "You're making it worse for yourself, you should have told your parents straight away, got it over and done with."

"But you know what they're like," Polly replied. "It'll be a nightmare if I tell them before I've got another proper job sorted out. Julie will never let me hear the end of it. I didn't imagine it would take so long for me to find another job."

"You'll find something brilliant soon, and maybe helping out with this farm will give you a creative outlet, something good to focus on until you're gainfully employed again. Plus, being solely in charge of a project would look great on your CV if your ideas pan out."

"You have a point . . ."

"If you really don't want to tell your family about losing your job yet, then stay off the subject when you're at the farm, you don't need to lie necessarily . . . Or could you say you're doing it as a freelance job, to keep the rates down as they're friends of the family?"

"Oh my goodness Alice, you're brilliant! That could work!" She grinned. "I knew there was a reason I was friends with you!"

"I'll watch the bar for you for a minute. Go and give them a call and tell them you've changed your mind. I've got a feeling this could be good for you."

"I will," said Polly, taking her mobile out of her back pocket. She was fed up with overthinking everything, and genuinely believed she'd be able to do some good at the farm, it was worth a try at least. "This could be just the challenge I need at the moment."

CHAPTER THREE

On Saturday afternoon, Polly was once again in her little car, driving back down to Kent, but feeling far more excited than the last time she'd done the trip.

She'd spent hours online researching everything she could about how farming worked, and, most importantly, how farms turned a profit. Taking into account the little bit she knew about John and his surly son, including their lack of farming experience and capital to put into the business to kick-start it again, she'd drawn up an action plan she believed should work. It would mean a lot of changes though. She just hoped John would trust her enough to implement them.

John had been thrilled to hear from Polly when she'd called from the pub and told him about her change of heart, though worried they'd be taking advantage if they accepted her offer of not paying her unless Polly's plans led to them making a profit. She was able to reassure him and skirt around the issue of her job at Streamline successfully, though doing so left a nasty taste in her mouth.

It was good to be focusing on something which interested her again. Polly knew it hadn't been her fault she'd lost her job: the company wanted to get rid of someone with her job description, and she was the last one hired so would cost them the least to get out; she hadn't actually done anything wrong. But that knowledge didn't make her feel any better about herself or her situation.

But at least she was feeling positive today and was much more prepared for the farm, wearing slightly too-big wellies borrowed from Alice, jeans and a thick jumper rather than her suit. John had invited her to stay for a couple of nights, so she could really get her teeth into things. Luckily she'd been able to rearrange her shifts at work without too much trouble.

As she entered the farmyard, remembering to close the gate behind her this time, John came out of the cowshed, wiping his hands on a rag. He smiled broadly at her, "Hello there," he called cheerfully. "Come on into the house, and we'll get the kettle on."

She followed him inside and John busied about with the kettle and finding biscuits. Polly wondered if he was a little nervous about what she had to say, or possibly how Mark would react.

"I'll give Mark a shout," John said, once the teas were made. "Back in a second."

Polly stood by the sink and watched him through the large window. John seemed to have the weight of the world on his shoulders as he walked slowly across the farmyard. He'd had such a hard time, she just hoped what she suggested would help him.

Mark didn't appear very impressed at being called in to hear Polly's plans.

"I was in the middle of putting up some fencing," he said grumpily. "I'll lose the light soon." He ignored Polly's presence completely, which she found unbelievably rude, but chose not to comment on. Two could play at that game, but she also didn't want to upset John.

"It's important we're both here to hear what Polly has to say," said John.

Mark humphed and sat opposite her. John passed his son a large mug of tea, then settled down himself.

Polly felt suddenly nervous as she realised the pair were waiting for her to begin speaking. They were effectively placing their home and their livelihood in her hands.

"So," she began, clearing her throat. "Obviously I haven't seen any actual figures for the last few years' accounts as yet, but going around the farm, and speaking to you, has given me an idea of the general picture, and what I think needs to be done.

"The first, and the biggest, thing is simply that the farm is too large for you to manage, and it would take years, and a lot of investment, to get it to the point where it could, potentially, make a profit."

"So you think we should sell?" asked Mark, gruffly. Polly looked up to meet his eyes. They were an intense grey she noticed, and she was sure she spotted a flicker of emotion in them.

"Not everything," replied Polly quickly. "And definitely not the yard or the farmhouse, or the cottages, but the outlying fields, yes."

"That land has been in my mother's family for years," said Mark, glaring at Polly.

"I appreciate that, but, from the sound of things, if you don't do something pretty drastic, you're going to end up losing the whole farm."

"How much do you think we need to sell?" John asked.

"I'd say about two-thirds judging by what I've seen," Polly replied. "I've marked it out here on this print-out," she continued, ignoring Mark's glares.

John leant over to look at the map Polly produced, Mark didn't.

"And how exactly are we supposed to make any money without land to farm?" asked Mark.

"You're not going to be doing the same type of farming," answered Polly. "With the money from the sale of the land, I'd suggest you do up the row of cottages you showed me, and then turn them into self-catering holiday lets. You said they're structurally sound, though they haven't been lived in for a while, so most of the work would be cosmetic."

John nodded in agreement, which gave Polly the impetus she needed to continue.

"You'll have more than enough space for the animals you currently have. Perhaps get a few goats as well," she continued. "Run the farm as a place for families to visit. Enlarge the market garden, as that's your expertise, John. Maybe have a Pick Your Own veg patch. Sell the farm produce from here, as well as possibly stocking some other local produce."

"That certainly sounds very different," said John, a little cautiously.

"You don't have to do all my suggestions, you might have some better of your own, but your strength is gardening, so play to that."

"I am rubbish at farming," admitted John, with a smile.

"No, you're not," said Polly and Mark together. They turned towards the other, but averted their eyes as soon as they met.

"I am. This plan makes more sense."

"But selling the land!" said Mark, his voice rising and his hands clenched on the table top.

"Means we can hopefully manage to hold onto the house and the animals we have left," John answered.

"You could also have a camping field and turn the small barn into a tearoom, which someone else would run," added Polly.

"You've certainly got a lot of ideas," John said, thoughtfully.

"I really need to see the accounts to get a better idea, but here's the predicted profit from selling the land I suggest at auction."

Polly slid a piece of paper with the figures on over to John. He looked at it and his eyes widened. He handed it to Mark, who glanced at it and passed it back to his father.

"My sister, Sue, deals with all the farm accounts," John explained. "I'll have a chat with her about getting them to you in the morning. She's coming round then anyway so you'll get to meet her."

"That sounds good," said Polly, pleased John at least appeared to be receptive to her ideas. Mark, however, was another matter.

"Do you mind if I ask exactly how much all these 'suggestions' are going to cost us? Dad said you'd be taking a percentage of everything we earn?" asked Mark, his arms firmly crossed around his body.

"I'll charge you absolutely nothing if what I advise doesn't work," Polly replied immediately, so grateful to Alice for this idea, but also anxious to ensure she didn't end up actually working for nothing. "You'll only pay me if you begin to make a profit."

"If?" Mark repeated.

"When," stated Polly firmly. She passed him the folder in which she'd set out her fees, which would simply be a small percentage of the profits made by the changes implemented thanks to her suggestions. "I've gone into more detail about what I've come up with so far in here."

Mark looked through it and grunted. Polly took this to mean he hadn't found anything to complain about.

Mark went back outside to finish off the fencing while Polly helped John with supper — thick, homemade potato and leek soup with a local sheep's milk cheese and dense brown bread to mop it up with.

By the time Mark had returned and they'd eaten the delicious food, it was late, and Polly, with a full tummy and in the warm kitchen, was finding it hard to stifle her yawns. It didn't help that, in order to be able to afford to take the time off for this trip to the country, Polly had worked in the pub until 1 a.m. and had then done a shift from 9 a.m. until 3 p.m. before leaving for the farm. She was exhausted.

A phone left on the huge pine Welsh dresser along one wall of the kitchen beeped, and John got up to check it.

"That was Sue," John said. "She'll be popping down tomorrow morning around ten."

"Great," said Polly. "It'll be good to chat with her and get the figures." Polly had to admit, she was intrigued to meet Sue, and to discover exactly what had been going on with the farm accounts. How could this woman have let things get so bad? How could she have allowed it to carry on for so long? Or, maybe Sue had tried to speak to John, to make him see how big a problem he was facing, but he'd been the one burying his head in the sand. It would be interesting to find out.

"You must be tired," said John kindly, as Polly attempted to hide another yawn. "Let me show you up to your room."

Polly couldn't help herself from looking across at Mark's scowling expression: even though it had been her original plan, she really didn't want to spend the night in the same house as him; they'd probably have to share a bathroom, and she could only imagine how embarrassing it would be to bump into each other in the middle of the night. If she hadn't been so tired and worried about upsetting John, she would have made her excuses and driven home.

Then she had an inspired idea. "Would it be alright if I stayed the night in one of the cottages? It would be good for me to get a feel for them."

John's eyebrows raised. "If that's what you'd like . . . they're a bit rough and ready though, as you saw before."

"I'll be ok," said Polly, with as much determination as she could muster. "It'll give me a chance to work out what needs doing to them."

John hesitated, looking concerned. "It's supposed to be nippy tonight . . . You'll be much more comfortable in the spare room here."

"I think it's a good idea," piped up Mark, unexpectedly.

"Really?" blurted out Polly.

"Oh, yes," Mark replied. "You'll get a real feel for farm life."

"Well, if you're sure . . ." said John. "We can head over there in a few minutes. Let me just find you a torch and some blankets."

Polly washed up while Mark went off to finish what-ever he'd been up to outside. He had a definite spring in his step and appeared to be doing his best to stop himself from laughing.

I'll show him, Polly thought to herself. I'll prove I'm more than capable of spending a night without the luxuries he clearly considers me reliant on. She'd been camping when she was in the Guides plenty of times. Anyway, she'd seen the cottages — they were a bit basic, true, but it would be good for her to spend the time in one to help her work out exactly how much work would need to be done to get them ready for the holidaymakers.

And avoid having to sleep in the same house as Mark.

* * *

John and Polly set off through the farmyard and along a little lane, guided by the beams of their torches. The night was cloudy, blocking out the moon completely. Polly's little case on wheels bumped noisily along the wonky, rocky path.

Polly stuck as close to John as she could without giving away how spooky she was finding the dark.

Her attention was distracted by a light coming from a small barn tucked behind the cowshed. "What's that?" Polly asked, gesturing with her torch. She hadn't noticed the build-ing before.

"Oh, that's Mark's workshop. He hasn't been in there much recently. It's good to see him using it again."

What on earth does he need a barn to himself for? Polly wondered. She'd check it out in the morning — it might be suitable for the indoor petting zoo she was considering, it looked like it could be large enough.

With her attention off the path, Polly stumbled but was saved from falling by John.

"Thank you," she said.

"You okay there?" John asked.

"I'm good," Polly reassured.

They reached the little row of labourer cottages, and John took a large bunch of keys from his pocket. He tried a few of them in the door to the first cottage until he found the right one. He removed the key from the keychain before handing it to Polly.

"Come on in," John said, leading the way into the hallway and switching on the lights. The inside of the cottage wasn't as bad as Polly had assumed it would be. It was clean and dry, though it smelt musty. She could envisage how pretty and cosy it could be with some work.

"This is the cottage our farm manager lived in," John explained. "The others aren't in such a good state."

It was freezing. Goodness only knew how long the heating had been off. The downstairs comprised of a narrow hallway, with a sitting room leading off it, through which was the kitchen/diner. Ideally, the kitchen would be updated, Polly thought, but that could probably wait for a while. John made sure the water was working and fiddled around turning the heating on, and then they went upstairs where there were two decent-sized bedrooms and a bathroom. Again, the bathroom was a bit old-fashioned, but nothing disastrous. A lick of paint, a good airing and a clean, and some nice soft furnishings, and this cottage would be a great holiday rental.

John felt a radiator and frowned. "It's not getting warm. Maybe it needs bleeding . . . Are you positive you want to spend the night here?"

"Absolutely, I'll be fine with all the blankets we've brought along," Polly reassured him.

"Alright," said John with a shrug. "There's no phone I'm afraid, and the mobile signal's a bit patchy, but you should be able to get a couple of bars outside the house."

A little shiver of panic slithered down Polly: she knew she was being silly, but she hadn't ever been in a situation like this before. She was torn when John then left, she needed him to go so that she didn't give in to her fears, but she felt very jittery now she was all alone.

She tried to distract herself by making up her bed for the night and unpacking what she'd need. She brushed her teeth, washed her face, and got into her pyjamas.

She settled down into the little nest she'd created for herself. Taking out her Kindle, it was clear John had been right, there was absolutely no signal.

Polly hadn't even managed a chapter of her book before she realised her device was almost out of charge. She steeled herself before facing the cold outside of the blankets again and wriggled back out, quickly finding her charger and plugging it in, only to find herself plunged into darkness as the electricity went off.

Polly felt her way back to the bed and lay down in the pitch black. She pulled her blankets up higher, almost covering her face. John had been right, it was really cold in this stupid cottage. She must be an idiot to have even contemplated staying here when there was a room ready and waiting for her in a lovely warm farmhouse, complete with working lights and plug sockets.

The dark here was . . . really bloody dark. So much darker than the nights in the city with all its light pollution. Rain poured down outside, pounding on the roof, and at least two loud drips echoed throughout the room. Polly hoped they were from outside the window, but she couldn't be sure.

Polly fumbled around for her phone so she could check the time. It was still only 10:30 p.m. An owl hooted, making her jump up to a sitting position. Why was she feeling so nervy? She was perfectly safe here . . . it was like the middle of nowhere. But would anyone be able to hear her if she screamed? Why would she even be thinking that? Of course they would, she was being stupid . . . she'd scream really loudly if some serial killer broke in and tried to murder her in this rickety bed.

Polly sank back down into the pillows. She was so tempted to give up and traipse back over to the farmhouse, but there were two things stopping her. Firstly, the thought of walking in the dark and rain by herself, and, secondly, the look on Mark's face when he was proved right about her not being able to manage a night in one of the cottages. She'd simply have to see it through.

Farmers were renowned for getting up early, so she'd get herself back over to the farm in only, what, eight and a half hours? She could last eight and a half hours.

* * *

Polly turned over and reached for her phone yet again — thank goodness, it was 6:30 a.m. She must have dozed off for the last few hours, when she'd last looked it had been 3:15 a.m.

Stretching as she glanced around the room in the faint morning light, there was no visible water damage from the rain. She pulled open the floral curtains: it was a misty, damp morning but, even so, the view from the back of the cottage was remarkable — rolling hills and green fields as far as the eye could see. It was beautiful. People would pay to stay here for that alone.

Polly tried the light switch with her fingers crossed, but the electricity was still out: maybe a line had come down in the bad weather?

Making her way into the bathroom, Polly dared a glance at herself. She was an absolute fright. Her hair looked like she'd been dragged through a hedge backwards after her night of tossing and turning, and the bags under her eyes would have been charged an excess by any airline. She couldn't head back over to the farmhouse in this state. Thank goodness there was a shower here and she had her make-up with her, even if she wouldn't be able to use her hairdryer and straightener without any electricity.

Polly shivered as she stripped off for the shower, hopping from one foot to the other on the icy, tiled bathroom floor. She stepped into the shower and turned the dial to hot. She gasped as she found herself pummelled with freezing cold water and leapt back out of the spray, peering at the dial to see if she'd set it on 'Arctic' by mistake: nope, it was on hot. Maybe it needed a minute or two to heat up. She waited, squeezed into the corner of the shower unit, as far away from the spray as she could get and held out her hand to test the temperature of the water. It remained icy. Finally, it dawned on Polly what the problem was: the shower was electric and, as the electricity wasn't working, there was no hot water.

Stoically concluding that at least the cold water would wake her up — and weren't cold showers supposed to be really good for you anyway? — Polly jumped back into the stream and washed as quickly as she could. Wrapping herself up in the large towel John had provided for her, she climbed back into bed to warm up. She dressed under the covers and stayed there while she'd put on her make-up in the grey early morning light, and did the best she could with her hair without her usual gadgetry.

Polly made some more notes on her plans for the farm while she impatiently urged the time on her watch to read at least 7 a.m. As soon as it was, she grabbed her belongings and left, unsurprised to find it felt warmer outside than in the cottage.

She was gasping for a cup of tea and assumed both John and Mark would be up early, but if she reached the farmhouse and it seemed they were both still asleep, she'd head back to the cottage for another hour or so.

She was in luck; smoke was unfurling from the farmhouse's chimney, and lights were on in the kitchen. She was spotted by John as she approached, and he waved cheerfully through the window.

The kitchen was warm and inviting, the kettle was just coming to a boil and the smell of toast made Polly's stomach growl.

Mark looked up from the pieces of paper he was reading. Polly noticed his mouth fall open. Could he have made it any more obvious that he'd considered her incapable of spending even an hour in one of the cottages without all the modern luxuries he clearly considered her obsessed with? Polly glared right back at him and considered herself victorious despite her cold, wet hair dripping down her back.

"How was the cottage?" John asked innocently, oblivious to anything other than the coffee he was pouring.

"A bit chilly," Polly admitted, ignoring Mark. "You were right about the radiators; they'll need bleeding at the very least. And the electricity went off last night."

"Did it come back on again?" asked Mark sharply.

"No," Polly replied.

Mark swore under his breath, pushed his chair away from the table, and stomped out of the room into the hallway. A moment later, they heard the front door slam behind him.

John sighed and handed Polly a cup of coffee.

"Sorry," she said. She wasn't really sure what she had to be sorry about, she hadn't done anything wrong, but felt bad that John was now dealing with the aftermath of her determination to stick to her guns and see the night in the cottage through. It had been a useful exercise in a way though — she knew a lot more about the property than she had before. And at least the problem with the electricity had been picked up now, by her, and not in the future by paying guests.

"Don't worry love, it's not your fault. He's a bit worked up this morning. We've got a couple of big bills coming up."

"Mind if I take a look?" Polly asked.

John looked embarrassed but slid the papers Mark had been frowning at over towards her.

"Is this on top of the other debts you told me about?"

"Yes."

Polly took out her notebook and jotted down the additional figures. Looking up again, the worry was plain on John's face, the lines deeper, and his eyes without their usual sparkle.

"I'm sure I can help," Polly said. "The first thing will be to get these debts under control."

Relief washed over John's face. "Well, we can't do that without a decent breakfast inside us."

"Absolutely," Polly replied, so glad that she'd made John feel better, temporarily at least. She just really hoped she'd be able to make good on her promises — even though she'd just started working with him, she couldn't bear the thought of letting him down.

* * *

After breakfast, Polly took her overnight bag upstairs to the guest room — one night in that cottage was more than enough. Even her stubborn head had to admit there was no point in her suffering through another freezing ordeal.

She tidied herself up, applying some more make-up and blow-drying and straightening her hair so she felt much more put together by the time she returned to the kitchen and found Mark eating his own breakfast.

"Hey," she greeted him awkwardly.

"Hey," Mark replied. "I checked on the cottage. The electricity seems to have been tripped. It's working fine now. Did you turn anything on, or plug anything in just before it happened?"

"Yes, I plugged my phone in to charge in the socket near the bed."

"That'll be it then. I'll call an electrician."

"Great — hopefully it won't be too expensive," Polly said. She received a grunt in reply.

"Well . . . I'm going to find your dad now. He said he'd talk me through the vegetable garden a bit more . . ."

"He'll be with the chickens," Mark muttered.

"Thanks," said Polly, moving towards the hallway as quickly as she could. She didn't think she'd ever met anyone so awkward and grumpy in her life.

It was a relief to be out in the fresh air — and the weather was doing its very best to clear up.

John showed her around his garden in more detail than he had on her first visit and she took some notes — she'd need to do more research, but John agreed he could definitely grow more if a lot of the farming work were taken off his shoulders. He loved her idea of a little farm shop in the yard.

The wide pathways between the beds would make the "market garden" perfect for visitors to explore and admire. John explained everything he'd done in the garden since he'd taken it over — it was clearly his pride and joy.

The squeak of the farm gate and sound of a car then driving through alerted Polly and John to Sue's arrival and they walked around the house to greet her.

Sue drove a spotless, pale-blue Ford Fiesta. When she emerged from it, she looked Polly up and down, appraising her with a faint sneer on her lips. Polly immediately got the impression that Sue, like Mark, didn't want her here.

"So, this is the famous London business guru is it?" she asked John.

"It is indeed," replied John, not rising to his sister's bait. He'd warned Polly the evening before that Sue could be a little "prickly", but he appeared to have made the understatement of the century. Was everyone here a grouch apart from John?

Sue was tall and thin, with brassy red hair nowhere near the colour of her eyebrows. The cream trousers and pale pink V-necked jumper she wore teamed with a pair of ivory coloured kitten heels were, even to Polly's untrained eye, quite supremely unsuitable for wearing on a visit to a farm, particularly one with such a mucky yard.

"It's good to meet you," said Polly, holding out her hand. Sue shook it limply.

"Let's get inside and pop the kettle on," suggested John.

* * *

When Sue departed a couple of hours later, Polly was left with no doubt that the woman strongly disapproved of her and her ideas for the farm. She'd reluctantly agreed to provide the accounts for the last few years, but hadn't been forthcoming about when she actually would send them over.

"Though I'm sure I don't know what you're expecting to find in them," Sue had said, grumpily.

She declined to stay for lunch, citing a previous engagement and Polly gave a little sigh of relief as the car drove off up the track and into the distance.

Mark disappeared after they'd eaten and John headed back into the garden with Dylan, after inviting Polly to wander around wherever she wanted. She felt more than a little awkward poking around someone else's property, but it was work, and John had been clear that she was welcome to go wherever she wanted.

Walking around the back of the cowshed, she spotted Mark's building again. Bravely, she knocked tentatively on the door. Part of her knew she was just being nosy, but she did also need to know exactly what each part of the property contained. There was no reply. She hesitated, then gave the door a little prod — it was unlocked and swung open.

Polly stepped inside. "Hello?" she called out. There was no response. Looking around, it was a stark contrast to the rest of the farm. It was immaculately tidy, set out perfectly with carpentry equipment and tools, and smelt lovely, of sawdust and beeswax. Polly wandered further in. A large workbench ran along the back of the space, with tools hanging neatly on the walls. There was a desk to the right, the piles of doodled on paper on it were probably the only messy part of the room. Pieces of wooden furniture in various states of disrepair or assemblage were dotted around. Mark seemed to do a mixture of restoring old pieces, and designing and building new. She absentmindedly ran her hands over an oak table — it was as smooth as silk — and picked up a chisel lying on the gleaming wood.

Suddenly, Polly realised she was not alone, she turned and found Mark standing behind her. He smelt of the fresh country air.

She jumped automatically. "I didn't hear you come in," she said. She felt flustered. He really was huge when he stood that close.

"Clearly."

Their eyes met. Polly looked away first. Mark's face was unreadable, but she was pretty sure he wasn't thrilled to see her. This was his private space, but if he didn't want anybody to come inside, he shouldn't leave it unlocked. And she did have permission to go around the property — she had to know what could be sold or used to make some much-needed money.

Mark's gaze fell to the tool in Polly's hand, and she held it out to him. He took it wordlessly. His hand brushed hers and sending a jolt through Polly's body. Mark jerked backwards — had he felt it too?

"Your dad said I could go wherever I wanted . . . I'm making notes and an inventory . . ." Polly found herself rambling.

"We're not selling my tools," Mark said firmly.

"No, of course not!" replied Polly, quickly. "Is this what you did before coming to the farm?"

"Yeah," Mark said quietly. "I had a workshop in Brighton."

"And you left it to work here with your father?" Polly asked awkwardly, moving away from the table.

"Yes, well my lease was up, and it was clear he needed me, so . . ."

"That was good of you, not all sons would give up their lives to help their dad."

Mark humphed and turned away, fiddling with some of the tools hanging on the wall.

"So, is everything in here to your satisfaction? Because I mean it, we're not selling my tools, they're not part of the farm's inventory," he said, still with his back to her.

"No, no," Polly reiterated hurriedly. "There's no need to sell any of this!"

"Good," Mark replied, shortly. "When I sell a completed piece, the money will, of course, go into the farm's account's accounts."

There was an awkward silence. Polly frantically searched her mind for something to say. Eventually, Mark said, "Well, if you've finished in here . . ."

"Oh yes, all done. I'll get out of your way."

Polly scurried off as quickly as she could, desperate to remove herself from the difficult situation. She heard the door shut behind her and let out a sigh of relief: how embarrassing — Mark appeared to view her as some sort of awful debt collector, not as someone who was trying to help!

She had to do something to improve relations between them, or things would only get worse once she tried to implement the changes she was planning — changes which now included putting Mark's woodworking skills to good use. But what could she do to get Mark more on her side?

CHAPTER FOUR

After an early supper of Cornish pasties from a local bakery and fresh winter salad leaves grown in the garden, Polly began talking John and Mark through her findings.

"I'm absolutely convinced that the key to getting this place back on its feet is to step away from traditional farming and focus more on your individual talents. For you, John, that's your gardening — stick with the farmer's markets, but increase the size of the garden so you can also sell your produce from a shop here. If you're going to have visitors, which I think you really should, a café would be a good idea, but have someone rent the café space from you — you can't do everything, and it will be a reliable source of income."

Neither John nor Mark seemed to hate what she was saying, or at least hadn't walked out yet, so she continued: "The first thing I believe you ought to work on is the row of cottages you showed me: they don't look to be in too bad a state, and you can begin renting them out without any of the other stuff here. Get them on Airbnb as each one is ready. Then you can concentrate on the things you're really good at and that you enjoy.

"There are a number of farms in the south of England which I've researched as case studies — they've made similar changes and have been successful, particularly when they had accommodation available for visitors. The important thing is to be original, to have something the other farms don't have . . ."

Polly was surprised to see Mark give a little nod of agreement.

"Actually, there's something I've been tinkering with which should be about ready," said John, mysteriously. "I'm hoping to be able to sell it at the farmer's markets."

"And what might it be?" asked Mark curiously.

"Follow me, and you'll find out," came the reply.

They got up from the table and John led them from the house, through the vegetable garden and to the big shed at the corner of it. Polly hadn't been inside there before; John had said it just contained the stuff he used for gardening. She made a mental note that it could at least do with a coat of paint before they began welcoming visitors.

The inside of the shed was like a snug little grotto: there were a couple of battered old armchairs, a table against one of the walls, a large, pretty lethal-looking heater, and a gas camping stove and kettle. At the very back of the shed was what John wanted to show them: an enormous traditional apple press and grinder. Next to it was a wooden barrel with a tap attached to the front.

"You made cider from the fruit in the orchard!" realised Polly, impressed.

"There were so many apples a couple of autumns ago — I sold some at the markets, but we still had hundreds left over. I found this old cider press and thought I'd give it a go. It should be well-aged by now."

"Are you sure it's safe?" asked Polly, sceptically.

John gave a chuckle. "It's just apples and yeast, it's perfectly safe."

He had some mugs by the camping stove and, picking up three of them, he poured them all a generous serving.

They clinked their cups together, and all took a deep glug of their drinks. A second later and they were all coughing and spluttering uncontrollably.

Polly was the first to regain the power of speech as she'd taken the smallest mouthful.

"That's . . . quite something!" she said diplomatically.

They all took another sip on reflex.

"It does sort of grow on you," said John, after a subtle clearing of his throat.

"I'm not sure this is really suitable for public consumption," Polly explained, as kindly as she could.

"Maybe you're right," John admitted. "Shame though."

"It's a great idea for this year's harvest if you can tweak the recipe a bit," Polly said, encouragingly.

Mark coughed. It sounded to Polly suspiciously like he was trying to cover up a laugh.

"That's very kind of you to say, love," said John, patting her on her shoulder. "Have a seat both of you." He sat himself on a stool he pulled out from under the table and indicated to the armchairs behind Polly and Mark. Mark immediately settled himself in one. Polly hesitated — the chairs were right next to each other, but she'd appear churlish if she declined the seat. She sat down but tried to keep her body as far from Mark's as she was able, without making it completely obvious what she was doing. How could he still smell so good after working on a farm all day? Dylan made himself comfortable in a basket in the corner.

"You've got it very well set up in here," commented Polly. "It's an ideal man cave."

"Yes, I've got my kettle and my biscuits, and my gardening books up there," John replied, pointing to a shelf full of books behind him. "All I need is a loo and I'd never have to leave," he added with another chuckle.

"I can usually find him hiding in here when there's mucking out to be done," commented Mark, sounding unusually affectionate.

"And you always hunt me down," John replied, wryly.

They chatted about the planned changes to the farm while they nursed their drinks until John, stifling a yawn, said, "It's getting late for me, and this stuff's making me

41

sleepy. I think I'll turn in for the night. You okay finishing up with the animals, son?"

"No problem, Dad," said Mark.

"See you in the morning," Polly said. "We'll check over the cottages and make a plan for the work on them before I head home."

"Lovely," John said. "Be sure to let Mark know if there's anything you need tonight."

Polly's cheeks flushed at the thought of sullen Mark's strong arms helping her off with her clothes. Where on earth had that thought come from? She was supposed to be concentrating on helping John, not lusting after his (admittedly ruggedly handsome) son. She didn't dare look at either man until she'd regained her composure, instead she kept her mug as close to her face as she could to hide it until she felt her colour return to normal.

John tottered off through the garden towards the house, a definite weave to his step. That cider was strong stuff.

Mark helped himself to another drink and indicated to Polly's empty mug. She deliberated: technically she was working here and so should stay professional, she was already a bit tipsy . . . but this was the first time Mark had been even vaguely approachable. He seemed to have let his guard down, at least to some extent, and she was eager to find out what he was like when he wasn't acting like a bear with a sore head.

She held out her cup for a refill. She was getting sleepy, and the shed was surprisingly cosy — one more drink wouldn't hurt. Maybe she could use the opportunity to break down some of Mark's remaining animosity. She felt she'd managed to crack through a little in his workshop earlier, but there was still a long way to go, and it seemed like the ideal time to make friends.

The second drink certainly went down easier than the first.

"I can't believe my dad actually thought he could sell this stuff," said Mark, with a shake of his head. "We'd end up being sued!"

"In fairness, he hadn't tried it when he suggested it," Polly replied. "And you do kind of get used to it."

"So, you reckon we'll make our millions selling it on tap in the farm shop then?"

"Maybe not." She smiled wryly. "I think your dad should probably stick to fruits and vegetables."

"I can't see fruits and vegetables making enough to clear our debts and be able to hang on to this place."

"I take it you're not convinced by my plan then?"

"I want to be," Mark said, with a sigh. He ruffled his dark hair and took another sip of his cider. "But I'm still not confident we can get out of this mess without selling the whole farm. And that would destroy Dad."

"I know it would," said Polly quietly, so grateful Mark was being honest and opening up to her, but also feeling guilty that she couldn't be as open about her own situation.

They were silent for a moment as they considered the ramifications of Polly's plan not working, something she'd been trying really hard not to do, because the more she got to know John, the greater the pressure she felt on herself. The ideas she'd been sketching out over the last few days could well be Nightingale Farm's last chance. She felt the weight of the responsibility.

"I do appreciate the effort you're putting into trying to help," Mark blurted out suddenly, his gaze meeting hers. Polly blushed as his eyes fell down to her lips before he looked away. Were his cheeks also reddening? What was going on here?

"Oh, thanks," replied Polly, her heart rate quickening. "It's my pleasure though."

"I can't imagine you spend this much time with all the businesses you work with."

Polly gave a noncommittal shrug. She desperately tried to think of a suitable change of conversation topic.

"Does your boss mind you being here?" Mark continued. "We wouldn't want you to get into trouble."

"It's fine," said Polly. "Your farm is sort of a special project for me."

"Well, I guess it feels good to have more of a purpose. We've been floundering around for a long time. As you've seen."

They both took a sip of their cider.

"It's wonderful here," Polly said.

"If you say so, though I think it's a little cramped," said Mark with a smile Polly couldn't help responding to with a grin of her own. It was the first time she'd seen a smile from Mark which reached his eyes. It made him seem far more approachable.

"Ha, ha," she responded. "I meant the farm."

"I know." He smiled again. Was he teasing her? "And you're right, it is wonderful. I've adored it my whole life. I used to love coming to stay here during the holidays when I was growing up. I spent every sun-filled day it seemed playing in the orchard with the local kids until my grandma called me in for a huge, home-cooked supper."

Polly was too shocked to reply for a moment: not only was this little speech the most she'd ever heard Mark say, but it was also by far the most emotion she'd ever seen him show.

"Sounds like you have good memories here," she said, finally.

"I do. But I've been worried that's all this place is: a collection of lovely memories with no real future."

"But you still moved here to help out your dad?"

"Of course. He needed me," said Mark, simply.

Polly nodded; she understood.

Mark refilled their mugs.

"Do you think this place can have a future now?" asked Polly, carefully.

"I think it could."

Polly gave an involuntary shiver; she hadn't realised how cold it had become in the little shed. Mark noticed and asked, "Shall we see if this heater works? Get ready to make a run for it if the wiring's a bit dodgy."

He rather gingerly turned on the heater. Slightly dusty smelling hot air began to emanate across the small space. It seemed safe, if a bit stinky, and it was nice to feel warmer.

"That's better," Mark said and sat back down next to Polly.

It really was getting late, but Polly was enjoying herself far too much to even think about going back to her room. She was so pleased she seemed to have had something of a breakthrough with Mark — turning the business round would be a lot easier if she felt she had Mark on her side.

And she realised she was finally, finally doing something she wanted to do. She could actually help a struggling business just like she'd always dreamed of doing. Not like when she'd been working at Streamline, where she'd felt pulled along by the ride and never able to do anything to rebuild rather than rip apart. And John was lovely — she was so anxious that her plans worked out for him.

Now she was warm and comfy in this shed, sitting in a scruffy old armchair with a mug of cider in her hand (disgusting cider, it was true, but she was in such a good mood, she'd decided to overlook that), and a very handsome man who seemed to have thawed to such an extent that he was positively charming. The only thing dampening her spirits was knowing she wasn't being entirely honest with John and Mark.

"So, is this how you spend all your Saturday nights?" Polly asked.

"This is about as exciting as it gets around here, but that's how I like it," Mark said. "The company's a little different tonight, but I could get used to that."

Polly grinned. "I'm glad."

She licked a drop of cider from her lips, feeling Joe's gaze on her.

They finished their drinks at the same time, downing the last dregs and turning towards each other. It must be well past both of their bedtimes and there wasn't an excuse to extend the evening any longer, but neither of them moved from there they were now sitting, which was much closer together than they had been.

"I suppose we ought to get back to the house," said Mark finally, standing up and offering a hand to Polly to aid her out of the chair she'd sunk into. Polly accepted his help and found herself rather closer to his chest than she had anticipated once she was standing. She dared a glance upwards. Mark was staring down at her, his grey eyes fixed on hers.

Polly took Mark's mug out of his hand and placed it by hers on the shelf next to them. She couldn't believe how brazen she was being: she was never usually like this, but there was no way she was going to stop now. She reached up slowly and tentatively kissed him, praying she wasn't reading the situation completely wrong.

Mark let out a low groan and began kissing her back, bringing her closer to him and running his fingers through her hair. Polly's knees felt weak and her hands were shaking with the intensity of what was going on in her body as she nudged him back onto the armchair before joining him, giving herself in completely to the moment. But then, suddenly, Mark pulled away from her and gently pushed her up.

"What's the matter?" Polly asked. Frustration coursed through her.

"I'm not sure this is a very good idea," Mark said, brushing his hair back from his face. "I don't know what came over me . . ."

"Right . . ." said Polly, feeling terribly embarrassed and vulnerable, and stepped back from him.

"I'm sorry . . ."

"Don't worry about it," Polly replied quickly. "Completely my fault. I should be getting to bed anyway. Got lots to do tomorrow."

Before he could say anything more, she turned and hurried out of the shed without looking back, nearly tripping in the dark. She stopped briefly to take out her phone from her back pocket and turned on its torch.

"Polly," she heard Mark call from behind her.

"I'm fine," she replied and carried on back into the farmhouse so she could hide in her room and try to forget the last few minutes had ever happened. How on earth was she going to be able to face Mark in the morning?

CHAPTER FIVE

Polly woke up with an absolutely pounding head and her throat dry and furry. She groaned as the memory of the previous evening hit her and she found herself feeling even more nauseous.

Nightingale Farm could be her big chance to get back en route to the career she had wanted for so long and had worked so hard for. Was she really going to risk all that for a roll in the hay with a handsome farmer? If it hadn't been for that awful cider, there's no way it would have happened. She never should have accepted one drink of the stuff, let alone a second and a third. What had she been thinking?

She couldn't have a relationship with a client, even if Mark wanted to, which it seemed he didn't. It was completely unethical. And then he'd felt the need to let her down so gently — how humiliating! He'd been such a gentleman — Polly couldn't help fancying him even more because of it. But there was no way she could sit opposite him at breakfast this morning. Presumably she'd have to work out how to be in the same room as him in the future without her face turning crimson, but she'd worry about that another time. One thing she knew for certain though: there was nothing, no matter how embarrassing, that would make her step away from helping Nightingale Farm and John.

But right now, what she needed to do was get out of the farmhouse and to her car without anyone noticing. She'd leave a note thanking John and Mark for their hospitality, but explaining that she unexpectedly had to get back to London earlier than planned. She could say she had another client she needed to meet. No. No more lies. Polly hated herself for misleading John and Mark as much as she had already. That had to be the end of anything dishonest, or at least any new dishonesty.

If spotted, her excuse would be that she wasn't feeling well — which was true enough. My goodness that cider had a lot to answer for!

Polly hid in her bedroom until she was sure both Mark and John had used the bathroom and gone downstairs. Then she slipped down the hallway, checking furtively over her shoulder to ensure she hadn't been spotted, and scuttled into the bathroom. She showered and dressed before returning to her room to pack. She heard the front door open and close and peeped around the curtain and through the window. John and Mark were talking together in the yard. She watched them, willing them to disperse and go about their business away from the house so she could slip away.

She wondered if they were speaking about her because at one point Mark looked straight up at her window and she had to quickly duck behind the curtain.

Finally, she had her chance: Mark wandered off in the direction of the cottages, and John to his garden. Polly grabbed her bags and launched her bid for freedom. She made it down the stairs and into the kitchen, but there she stopped. Breakfast things had been left out for her, tea was being kept warm in a pot under a thick tea cosy. A note lay beside it:

Hope you slept well. Help yourself to breakfast. I'll be in the garden when you're done. John

Polly smiled: what had she been thinking? She couldn't leave without speaking to John, she couldn't hurt his feelings like that after he'd been so open and generous to her. What sort of repayment for his kindness would that be?

Polly took her stuff out to the car and loaded it in. She was still very tempted to hop in herself but knew she'd feel terrible if she did. She must say goodbye to John; she prayed Mark was nowhere near, she absolutely couldn't cope with coming face-to-face with him this morning.

Walking around the house to John's garden, Polly couldn't see him amongst the beds. She was turning to leave the garden and begin a search for John further afield when she heard noises coming from the shed. She walked over and knocked on the door: she was pretty certain John would be by himself in there as she'd seen Mark heading off in the opposite direction, but she couldn't be a hundred per cent sure.

A muffled call of "Just a minute!" made its way to her, and a moment later John opened the door.

Polly let out a little sigh of relief and then felt her cheeks redden as she saw the chairs and the mugs left out from the night before.

"Hello!" said John, a touch too loudly for Polly's sore head. "Did you sleep well? You look a bit peaky. We missed you at breakfast."

"I slept well, thank you, but I'm not feeling too great this morning."

"That cider packs a punch," admitted John.

Polly smiled. "I'm sure it's not that. But I could do with resting up for the rest of the day, so I thought I'd head off now. I think we covered just about everything yesterday though, and I'll be in touch via email."

"I'm no good with email," John replied, "but Mark'll pick up anything you send."

Polly made a mental note not to send emails unless she absolutely had to.

"Thank you so much for your hospitality," she said. "It's been wonderful staying here and getting to know the place."

"No problem at all, it's been a pleasure having you. Are you sure you're okay driving yourself back if you're not feeling a hundred per cent?"

"Absolutely," said Polly.

John wiped his hands on a nearby tea towel and pulled her into a warm, heartfelt hug. "Don't stay away too long."

"I won't," said Polly, touched, but desperate to get away before Mark made an appearance. "You'll hear from me soon."

Hurrying to her car, Polly checked over her shoulder anxiously — she made it and even managed to close the gate behind her. She congratulated herself on her swift getaway but ignored the fact that part of her was hoping Mark would make an appearance and beg her to stay.

As she drove carefully down the windy country lanes leading from the farm down to the A road, a tractor approached in the distance, and Polly pulled over into a passing spot to allow it to go by. Lost in her thoughts, she didn't notice who the driver was until the vehicle slowed to a stop and Mark rolled the window down.

"Are you leaving already?" he asked.

Damn, Polly thought. Her face reddening, she managed to murmur, "Yeah, I think I've got everything I need, and I'm not feeling great."

Mark nodded. "About last night . . ." he began.

Polly interrupted, "I want to apologise about that," she said quickly. "It was completely unprofessional of me. The cider . . ."

"Was very strong," Mark finished for her.

"It certainly was," Polly replied, with a grateful smile. Mark opened his mouth to respond but was interrupted by a horn beeping behind him. A red-faced man was apparently losing his temper with this hold-up slowing down his journey.

Mark gave Polly an apologetic shrug and raised his arm cheerfully to the bad-tempered driver to signal he was sorry.

The tractor drove off back towards the farm, closely followed by the red-faced man's car, and Polly continued on her journey, knowing she was doing the right thing by leaving, but really wishing she didn't feel she had to and that the events of the previous night had never happened.

* * *

A few days later Polly had an evening off from the pub and was taking the opportunity to have a catch-up with Alice. It wasn't until they'd made their way onto their second bottle of Sauvignon Blanc and were properly settled on Alice's ancient, blanket-covered futon and easing stomachs full of huge bowls of cheesy pasta by administering handfuls of Maltesers, that Polly got up the nerve to confess what had happened between her and Mark.

"Mark, the farmer's bad-tempered son?" enquired Alice, with a twinkle in her eye. "So did you . . ."

"No!" Polly exclaimed, then admitted, "He stopped things before they went any further than kissing." She put her face in her hands, cringing at the memory.

"Then what happened?" Alice asked, sympathetically.

"He said he didn't think it was a good idea, and I made a super quick exit, and went to hide in my bedroom."

"Did you see him again before you left?"

"Very briefly. He was lovely about it, but it's so embarrassing. I practically threw myself at the poor man."

"I'm sure he didn't see it like that," her friend said kindly.

"I can't believe how stupid I was. I was finally beginning to win him round, he was actually starting to believe some of my ideas were worth trying, and I went and drank too much dodgy cider and ruined it all."

"You didn't ruin anything. He probably just felt awkward because you guys are working together. He's most likely kicking himself for turning you down."

Polly gave a little smile, she appreciated her friend's reassurance, and it did make her feel ever so slightly better about the situation.

"I'm not convinced about the kicking himself bit, but I hope that a bit of time apart will make it easier for me to be in the same room as Mark without blushing as red as a beetroot." Polly sighed and took a deep glug of her wine. "I so want this job to work out, not just for me, but for John as well. He's so nice, and I'd hate for him to lose the farm. It means such a lot to him."

"Your ideas are fantastic," Alice replied. "And you said Mark liked them. He wants what's best for the farm as well."

"You're right," admitted Polly.

"You can carry on the work remotely, can't you? At least for the time being, until you're happier about facing Mark."

Polly nodded. "Yeah."

"Well, do that then," concluded Alice. "You'll do a great job. If you quit because you feel awkward, that could be the end of the farm, couldn't it? John would lose his livelihood and have to sell his home. Try to forget about what happened and do the best you can to help that business."

* * *

Polly hadn't been in the mood for a late night, especially as she was opening up in the pub the next morning, so she was back at her flat making herself a chamomile tea by 10 p.m. She climbed into bed with her book, but was too distracted to be able to concentrate and her mind kept wandering back to what Alice had said.

Polly knew her friend was right: Polly had messed up, but there was no reason that should impact her work. She only wished she could stop thinking about that kiss and wondering what would have happened if Mark hadn't pulled away when he did. She knew she wouldn't have been capable of stopping if it had been up to her. And he'd seemed to be enjoying it as much as she had . . .

She was more humiliated than anything — not only for being seen to let her guard down and being so unprofessional, but more by the fact that Mark had rebuffed her.

Why did she have to get a stupid crush on him of all people? They didn't even have anything in common. Yet Polly had to admit there was something about him . . . even when he was being grumpy and sullen.

He was certainly good-looking, there was no denying that, but he also appeared to be a genuinely good person beneath his bad moods — Polly could still hardly believe that he'd give up his own business and way of life to move into the farmhouse and help his dad. It was admirable. There was also something very attractive about the fact that he worked with his hands — what she'd seen of his carpentry was beautiful, and even her untrained eyes could see he was very skilled at what he did. He wasn't someone who pretended they liked you when they didn't. And she liked how she'd had to win his trust — albeit even if she did have to spend a night in a rundown farm cottage to do so.

But he'd made it abundantly clear that he wasn't interested in her. She needed to focus on helping the farm and forget what had happened between them. If she managed to pull this off, not only would she make some money, but she'd finally be on track to doing something she loved.

If she were honest, as crushed as she'd been to have lost it, her old career hadn't been everything she'd hoped for — she wanted to help businesses, to save jobs, and make things work more effectively. Instead she'd been instructed to break up businesses in the cheapest, quickest way possible. It was often a lot easier to let a struggling company go and for the directors to start afresh than to put the effort into trying to save it.

Nightingale Farm was truly special, it had taken her spending less than a day there to realise that, and had a history and importance to John and Mark. She had to do everything she could to help them. She'd just have to focus on that and not the feeling of Mark's arms around her and his lips on hers.

* * *

The next four weeks went by in a blur for Polly — if she wasn't taking on as many shifts as possible at the Bluebell, she was working on her plans for Nightingale Farm, which always seemed to be on her mind. Emails went back and forth between her and John. She was all too aware that Mark would also be reading this correspondence, and so spent an inordinate amount of time checking over and unnecessarily rewording what she'd written before she sent it.

To her delight, the farm's debts had been consolidated, and the parcels of land set aside to be sold were going to auction in a few days. There had been a lot of interest and the auction house was confident they would fetch a good price, which would really ease things financially for the farm.

John reassured her that things were moving forward well with the various new ventures, and had attached some photos of the outside of the cottages to the emails, which Mark had presumably helped him to send. John had tidied up the little front gardens, the windows had been washed, and the doors given a fresh coat of paint. A roofer had been to replace a couple of loose tiles and unblock some guttering.

A little meadow next to what would be the camping field was being prepared to be a play area for visiting children, and a large pumpkin patch and Pick Your Own Strawberries field were prepared and ready to be planted in a couple of months.

It was Friday afternoon, and Polly was researching the costs of setting up a Christmas tree paddock — it should bring in extra visitors for the season, but it would take a while for the trees to establish and be large enough to cut . . . Maybe they could plant them and have a Winter Fair this year, people would like to see the newly planted trees, and they could serve mulled wine and have craft stalls. Could they hire a couple of reindeer? Maybe Mark could whip up a sleigh for Santa in his workshop . . .

Polly's thoughts were interrupted by her mobile ringing, she picked it up and saw it was the farm's phone number. She was pretty sure it would be John calling, but she still steeled herself in case it was Mark.

The tiny sigh she let out at hearing John's voice when she answered was a mixture of relief, and a little bit of disappointment.

"Hello, Polly," John said, chirpily. "How are you?"

"I'm good, thanks. I was working on the costings for the Christmas trees. How's everything at the farm?"

"I'm hoping you'll be rather impressed with what we've managed to do. Any chance you could pop down and take a look?"

Polly had been putting off going to the farm, but she knew she couldn't any longer. If they had any chance of getting at least some of their plans up and running for the summer, they really needed to be on top of things. Plus, she had to admit, she was dying to see how they'd been getting on in person.

"I can come tomorrow if that suits you?" A couple of the other bartenders at the pub owed her shifts she could call in to cover her for the weekend.

"Wonderful! You'll stay the night, won't you? Sue should be coming on Sunday, and it would be good for the two of you to spend some time together . . ."

"That sounds great," Polly said, trying to be positive at the prospect of another awkward meeting with awful Aunt Sue. "I can be with you by lunchtime."

"See you then!" John said, happily. "I think you'll be pleasantly surprised. I can't believe how much we've done since you were last here."

Polly couldn't help the smile on her face when she got off the phone: despite her feelings for Mark, it would be so lovely to get back to Nightingale Farm. Now she just had to work out what she was going to wear so that she felt as confident and in control as possible when she saw him.

* * *

The sun was doing its best to shine through the clouds as Polly's car pulled into the farmyard the next day.

She was immediately struck by the difference in the state of the yard: it was pristine, nothing like the first time she'd visited. The fences were repaired, as were the chicken coops, and the pile of old machinery had been removed.

John appeared from behind the house — he must have been working in his garden — closely followed by Dylan, who was as thrilled to see Polly again as she was him.

Polly was enveloped in a hug as soon as John reached her.

"The yard!" she said, excitedly. "It looks fantastic!"

"That was all Mark," John admitted with a smile, "But don't worry, I've done plenty too. We'll have a cuppa before I take you around. I'm parched."

Polly followed John into the house and felt her whole body relax as she sank down into the chair by the Aga. Dylan lay himself down by her feet and John poured her a cup of tea from the pot on the table. If only her own home made her feel the way this kitchen did.

"We've missed seeing you," said John. "It's good to have you back here."

"It's good to be back," Polly answered, honestly. "How's everything coming along?"

"Really well — I hope you'll be impressed," John said. "Not having to worry about doing anything with the land that's being sold off has really freed up Mark's time."

"Has he been able to work on his carpentry more?" Polly asked.

"Oh yes," replied John with a grin.

Polly downed her drink as quickly as she could. She was excited to see all the changes that had been made straight away, but anxiety about seeing Mark again was doing its best to overwhelm her. Her stomach was churning as she played out their looming meeting in her mind on an endless reel.

"Mark's just finishing off something. He'll meet us at the cottages," John said, saving Polly from having to ask. His face made it completely plain that he had something special to surprise her with.

The weather outside was turning grey and a bit drizzly, but Polly was now an old hat at farm life with her North Face Triclimate jacket and wellington boots, all lucky charity shop finds.

Even in the miserable weather, the change in the exteriors of the cottages was immediately apparent when they came into view. They looked so much fresher and cleaner, more inviting. The front gardens were neat and tidy, and the gates freshly painted, as was the front door and the window sills and surrounds.

"Wow!" Polly said, "You've done a brilliant job! They look even better than in the photos you sent!"

"Wait until you see inside," said John, with a smile. He went through the gate to the cottage Polly had stayed in and held it open for her to follow him, then led her to the front door which swung open at his touch.

"Mark!" John called out. "Polly's here!"

Polly prepared herself to see Mark again, making sure she stood tall and confidently — she didn't want him to realise how nervous she was.

Polly failed to immediately notice how different the inside of the house looked because she was so focused on Mark's appearance. The man himself emerged from the kitchen, wiping his hands on a cloth. Damn it, he was handsome, even wearing old jeans and a pale-blue wool jumper which had definitely seen better days.

"Welcome back," he said to Polly, in a far friendlier manner than she was used to him greeting her, but meeting her eyes only fleetingly.

It was then that Polly properly took in the change in the cottage: the walls had all been given a fresh coat of paint and carpets had been removed to reveal the original pine floorboards, polished to perfection.

Seeing the disbelief on Polly's face, John said, "Go on, look around properly!"

John and Mark moved out of Polly's way, and she walked into the sitting room. The fussy, yellowing nets had been replaced with smart Venetian blinds, and the walls were pale grey. An oak coffee table was positioned in the middle of the room, presumably waiting for a sofa to join it. The same style of wood had been used to build some bookshelves in an alcove next to the kitchen's entranceway. Polly suspected they were Mark's handiwork.

The kitchen had also been vastly improved — the lino had been replaced with slate tiles and the cupboard doors had been updated, as had the countertops, which carried on the oak theme from the sitting room. Mark must have worked incredibly hard to get so much carpentry done in such a short space of time.

"You made these," Polly stated simply, looking Mark straight in the eyes — she needed to prove to him, and to herself, that she could be professional and that there would be no problem with them working together. "How did you do everything so quickly?"

Mark smiled and shrugged. "The coffee table was already made, and the wood for the shelving was basically cut. The counters in here were a bit trickier," he admitted, running his hand over the wood.

"And it's warm!" Polly exclaimed, realising that was another reason why the cottage now felt so much nicer.

"Yeah," said Mark. "I bled all the radiators and we had the boiler serviced. Fingers crossed, it seems to be working fine now."

"You've done a huge amount," Polly said.

"It's only this cottage that's nearly ready," said Mark quickly. "There wasn't any proper renovation work to do."

"We made sure we kept all the receipts," piped in John.

"It all looks wonderful," Polly exclaimed.

"There's some furniture to pick up to finish it off. I've got a budget, and I'm going to Ikea tomorrow," said John.

"That's great. If we get it in place when you get back, I should be able to take some photos for the Airbnb listing while I'm here," said Polly.

"I've looked online and chosen everything we need," John said, "And I've got use of a van for the day."

"A woman named Maggie's van," added in Mark, with a conspiratorial wink to Polly which, despite all her promises to herself to keep her distance from this man, made her stomach dance with happiness. "And she's going with him."

Poor John blushed bright red. "She's been to Ikea before so she knows all about that convoluted system they have for how to get around it, and she needs a bedside lamp."

"Who's Maggie?" asked Polly, enjoying obligingly picking up on Mark's cue.

"Maggie is the lady who's going to be running the café," said Mark. "She and Dad have really hit it off."

"That's good to hear," Polly said, doing her very best to hide her smile; she didn't want to embarrass John more than he already was, but it was lovely to think that he and this Maggie were getting on so well. Polly was already looking forward to meeting her.

"She's a nice lady and her cakes are delicious. She should do a grand job with the café," said John quietly, as a firm end to the subject. "Come and see upstairs," he suggested. "We changed the flooring up there as well. We decided not to pull out the old bathroom suite as it would be pricey, and it can always be changed at a later date, but we freshened the room up."

* * *

Once they'd shown Polly the rest of the house they took her down to see the progress on the Pick Your Own field and the pumpkin patch.

"Show her the hedges, Dad," encouraged Mark as they began making their way back to the house.

John looked doubtful, and rubbed his neck the way Polly had noticed Mark did when he was nervous.

"Go on. They're brilliant," Mark encouraged.

Polly followed them round to where the children's play area was going to be. One side of the paddock had a large hedge growing alongside it. Polly was amazed by how it had been transformed and whipped out her phone straight away to take some snaps for the new Instagram account she was setting up for the farm. The whole hedge had been trimmed to make a parade of farm animals, ranging from a cow at one end down to a chicken at the other. It was an inspired idea, and Polly was so proud of John for thinking of it and executing it so well. She was sure it would be a big hit with the families visiting when they opened to the public on the weekends in only a few weeks' time. Now she had to focus on making sure she spread the news of what they were doing far and wide so they had plenty of people queuing up to experience everything Nightingale Farm had to offer.

CHAPTER SIX

Polly had been asleep in the little antique single bed in the farmhouse's spare bedroom for a while when she was woken suddenly by a noise from downstairs. She checked the time on her mobile, it was just after 1 a.m. John and Mark had turned in hours ago she knew. Maybe one of them had popped downstairs for a glass of water.

She waited a moment or two, listening intently. There was a muffled bump. What if someone was breaking in? Shouldn't she go and check everything was alright? And actually, now that she was awake, she realised she was thirsty. She wouldn't be able to get back to sleep if she didn't reassure herself that John and Mark weren't being robbed blind, but she'd use the pretence of needing a drink because she knew she was most likely overreacting.

She heaved herself out of bed and pulled on some socks, the tiled kitchen floor would be chilly on bare feet.

Polly slipped down the windy stone staircase as quietly as she possibly could, feeling her way in the dark: if there actually was a burglar in the kitchen she wanted to surprise them. She planned to pick up a poker from the living room fireplace as she passed it — just in case.

Her worry was needless she realised when she heard the kettle boiling as she reached the bottom step. She'd never heard of any criminal making themselves a warming beverage as they collected up valuables.

The light was on in the kitchen and Mark stood by the kettle. He was bundled up in a big coat and hat. A pile of old towels was on the table and Mark was talking on the telephone.

"Okay, thanks. I'll see you soon," he said, finishing the call.

He turned and gave a start when he saw Polly. She performed a little wave. Why did she do that? Who did she think she was? The Queen?

"Oh, hi," he said. "Sorry, did I wake you?"

"It's fine," Polly said, quickly. "I needed a drink anyway. Is everything alright?"

"Barbara is having trouble lambing."

"Barbara?"

"One of our ewes," replied Mark, the tips of his ears turning pink. "I went out to check on her before heading to bed. She was lambing so I stayed with her, but she got into difficulties. That was the vet on the phone, he's on his way."

"Is there anything I can do to help?" Polly asked, instinctively. She was hardly a sheep expert, but she couldn't bear to think of the animal in pain, and things must be serious if Mark was calling the vet out in the middle of the night — she'd seen how large some of the farm's out of hours vet bills could be.

Mark hesitated. Polly couldn't blame him, she wouldn't be her own first choice to help a ewe through a difficult birth either. He looked at her, seeming to size her up for the task.

"Sure," he answered finally. "Put on your coat and some wellies and grab those towels."

Polly did as she was instructed. Mark disinfected the plastic washing up bowl before filling it with boiling water and they quickly made their way outside to the animal shed.

The cries of the struggling ewe hit Polly's ears long before they reached her and wrenched at Polly's heart. A large part of her wanted to spin right around and go back to the nice warm farmhouse, but she wouldn't abandon Mark, who looked just as petrified by what was going on as she did.

Mark had left the lights on in the shed when he'd left to call the vet. They both washed their hands at the sink by the door before slipping inside. There were a few cows and sheep in stalls dotted along the side of the building. Barbara's stall was tucked away in the far corner, and the ewe was right up at the back of it. She had plenty of clean straw around her and a bucket of water, but was obviously in some distress. Mark got down next to her and stroked her head, speaking quietly and gently into her ear which seemed to calm the animal.

"What can I do?" Polly asked.

"Would you wait by the gate for the vet to arrive?" Mark asked. "He should be here soon."

She nodded. "Holler if you need anything," she said.

Polly walked back outside and made her way to the farm's gate. She'd closed the shed's door behind her so as much heat as possible stayed inside it. This had the unfortunate effect of also cutting off the majority of her light source.

She pulled her coat closer around her and stamped her feet to keep warm, her eyes glued to the track leading up to the farm.

She could make out poor Barbara's bleating as well as noises from the other animals nearby, but, other than that, the night was quiet.

It could only have been about five minutes later that Polly spotted headlights approaching. She opened the gate in readiness, and the vet waved his thanks as he drove through. Dylan began barking in the house and Polly willed him to stop, she didn't want the noise to upset Barbara further. Thankfully he went quiet again.

Once the gate was securely shut again, Polly went to join Mark and the vet. They were huddled around Barbara. Polly tried to read from their faces how things were looking, but couldn't work it out. Mark looked round and caught her eye. "Could you hold her head still and talk to her?"

"Sure," Polly replied and took up her position before wondering what on earth she was going to talk to a labouring sheep about.

"She's not doing well," the vet said grimly. "It's going to have to be a caesarean section I'm afraid, I'll need to give her a local anaesthetic and get these lambs out fast if we have any chance of all three surviving this."

"She's having twins?" Polly said.

"Yes," Mark replied. "It seems they're a bit tangled up in there."

Polly averted her eyes from the vet's preparations, concentrating on trying to speak calmly to Barbara. "Your babies will be here soon," she said soothingly. "Everything's going to be fine."

She glanced up and caught Mark looking at her. She blushed, embarrassed. Realising he'd made her feel uncomfortable, he said, "You're doing great. Thank you."

Polly gave him a little smile in response — his reaction gave her the impetus she needed to keep talking to the poor ewe. She focused completely on reassuring the animal and helping her through the pain. It was mere moments until she heard the vet say, "Here's the first one." He placed the little bundle next to Barbara who began to feebly lick her baby.

Mark swooped in. He squeezed the lamb's nose to clear its nostrils out and then began rubbing the animal with a handful of straw.

Polly saw the lamb take a deep breath and it gave a little bleat. She breathed a sigh of relief.

The next lamb took longer to extract. "Mark," the vet said calmly. "The ewe's losing a lot of blood and I'm struggling to get the second lamb. I'm going to have to make a bigger incision and I need you to staunch the blood as much as you can."

"Are we going to lose her?" asked Mark, his furrowed brow betraying his emotion to Polly.

"We will if we can't get this lamb out."

Polly stayed out of the way, ready to help if needed. She wished there was something she could do. Maybe then the seconds wouldn't seem to last as long as they were.

"And number two," said the vet finally. The second lamb was pulled out and placed next to its sibling. It was still and silent. Polly felt her stomach drop as she watched Mark go through the same manoeuvre as he'd used on the first lamb without any success this time. The vet stayed calm. "Mark, I need you back over here. Polly, can you give her a rub with some straw like Mark did?" he asked. "Let's see if we can get her moving."

Polly grabbed hold of some of the cleaner straw next to her and began gingerly stroking the lamb. "You'll need to be a bit rougher," Mark grunted, shifting his focus briefly to her before returning it to helping the vet who had already removed the afterbirth, and was beginning to stitch up Barbara. Polly tried to recall anything she might have seen or read about how to do this; nothing was coming to mind. She moved closer to the lamb and began rubbing it more vigorously, but there was still no sign of life.

"Pick it up by the back legs and swing it gently," the vet instructed. "The gravity helps to clear the airway. It would usually be done as the lamb is pushed through the birth canal, but with a c-section, they often need a little more help."

Polly gulped. It was definitely better not to overthink this. She took hold of the lamb's back legs. They were so slippery, she had to tighten her grip. Holding it upside down, she swung it from side to side just as the vet had said.

"Okay, now check the nose is clear and try rubbing her again," said the vet.

Polly lay the lamb back down and squeezed its nose before she began rubbing again, her own heart pounding in her chest. Suddenly the lamb made a little noise, like a cough, and began to breathe. Polly felt tears pooling in her eyes. She watched as both lambs began attempting to stand up just a few minutes later.

"Well done, Polly," said Mark. "What's the prognosis with the ewe, Jack?"

"She's all stitched up," the vet replied. "With rest, I think she should be fine. You did a good job slowing her blood loss. I'd only recommend a transfusion if she doesn't show signs of perking up in the next couple of days. She'll need to be checked on regularly, any sign of infection, call me straight away."

* * *

When the vet was satisfied with how all the animals were doing, Polly and Mark helped him carry his stuff to his car.

"The mother won't be strong enough to feed her lambs to begin with, they'll have to be bottle-fed," explained the vet. "I'll leave you some colostrum replacer which they'll need now and for the first few feeds, then you'll need to get them formula."

"That's not a problem," said Mark.

"I'll pop back this afternoon to check how they're getting on. Give me a call if the ewe goes downhill, but I'm confident she'll be fine."

"Thanks," Mark said, shaking his hand, the relief plain to see on his face. "You get inside," he said to Polly. "I'll sort out the gate."

Polly didn't need telling twice, it was really cold out in the yard.

* * *

Once the vet had left, Mark found some bottles and Polly went back to the house to wash them properly with a bottle brush at the kitchen sink while Mark cleaned up around Barbara and her lambs.

When she returned to the shed, Mark made up the feed left by the vet and Polly and Mark sat side by side on up-turned buckets feeding the lambs. He showed her how to hold the bottle up so the lamb didn't take it in too much air. They sucked hungrily.

"They need names," declared Polly.

"What do you suggest?" Mark asked, looking amused.

Polly stroked the female lamb on her lap. Bubbles of milk escaped from the corners of her mouth as she put all her efforts into drinking.

"Bubble," Polly decided.

"Bubble? Really?" Mark wrinkled up his nose in disgust.

"Well, what would you call her?"

"Not Bubble."

Polly decided to ignore him. She looked at Mark's lamb, trying to think of a suitable name. Mark removed the bottle from her mouth for a moment and the lamb let out an indignant, high-pitched whine. "And the other one is Squeak," Polly decided.

Mark signed in resignation.

They put some heat lamps on and made sure the lambs were warm and comfortable next to their mother.

Barbara lay quietly. Mark brushed the top of her head as they left, and murmured something in her ear. As they headed back to the farmhouse, Polly felt a lump in her throat at how tender this man was with the animals he cared for. If he hadn't been so vigilant, and called the vet out despite the cost, it was very unlikely that Barbara or her twins would have survived.

* * *

It was 5 a.m. on the kitchen clock when Mark and Polly got back inside.

Mark sat down heavily on a kitchen chair.

"Would you like a cup of tea?" Polly asked. He looked exhausted.

"I think I'll just try to get some sleep on the sofa. I'll need to be up again in a couple of hours to feed the lambs and check on Barbara."

He bent down and began untying the laces on his boots.

"Thanks for your help," he said, quietly. Polly would have missed it if she hadn't been paying such close attention to him.

"It was my pleasure."

"It was good to have you there. I know it's silly to worry so much about a ewe, but Barbara was my mother's. She reared her by hand before she became ill, and Barbara would follow her around the farmyard like a dog. I'd never sell her or her offspring, so the vet's bills won't be made back at market on Barbara or her lambs."

Polly nodded, she understood.

Mark was so different to how he had first come across. All the gruffness was a shield he hid behind because of the worry and hurt he was dealing with every day as he tried his best to run a large farm without the expertise and the help he needed.

"Bubble and Squeak will be the star attractions when we open to the public," Polly said. "They'll more than pay their way with how cute they are."

"That's true," agreed Mark. "Kids will love to cuddle them at Easter."

Polly felt suddenly overcome with tiredness and the need to process all the emotions flooding through her. Now that all the excitement was over, she was also acutely aware that she was wearing her pyjamas. "I'll get back to bed then."

"Sure," Mark replied. "See you later."

* * *

Polly fell asleep again almost as soon as her head hit the pillow, but she had set an alarm for eight, she wanted to help feed the lambs.

When the alarm went off, she got out of bed and pulled on some tracksuit bottoms and a hoodie before quietly going downstairs. Mark was asleep on the sofa, his brow creased with worry. Polly felt an urge to stroke it, to help him relax and trust that she was helping with the situation and that it was getting better, but she managed to stop herself. Instead, she pulled the blanket he had over him up a bit higher so he didn't get cold.

John was in the kitchen finishing off his breakfast.

"I hear you had a busy night of it," he said, smiling as Polly walked in.

"You could say that, but Mark did much more than I did. Do you know how they're doing?"

"Both lambs are doing well, and we're hoping to get Barbara up and moving later today. Fingers crossed, she'll be able to take over feeding them herself before too long."

"She's certainly a resilient girl," Polly commented.

"She is. I'm so grateful to you both for helping her."

"It was my pleasure, and quite the education," said Polly with a laugh.

A rather groggy-looking Mark entered the kitchen. "Is the kettle hot?" he murmured.

"Course it is, son," said John. "I'll sort you out with a coffee."

"Thanks, Dad," Mark said, sitting down heavily on a chair opposite Polly.

"You can sleep for longer if you like," Polly suggested. "I'm happy to do the next lot of feeds for you."

"Thank you," Mark said, looking up at her. "But I've got other jobs to do around the farm anyway. I'd appreciate a hand though." Turning his attention to his dad, Mark said, "Polly was great last night. I honestly couldn't have managed without her."

"I'm sure she was," John replied. He left to tend to his garden with a smile on his face.

"Why are you being so nice?" Polly couldn't seem to stop herself from blurting out once John was out of earshot. "It's . . . sort of weird."

Mark frowned at her. "Weird?"

"Why are you being nice?" Polly repeated.

"You were a big help, I was just stating a fact. And anyway, I'm a nice guy, it's normal for me to be nice."

"But you can be kind of grumpy . . ."

That comment got a smile from Mark. "Dad thought I'd upset you by being 'kind of grumpy' as you put it," he admitted. "He accused me of being the reason you've been staying away."

Polly managed to stifle the laugh threatening to bubble up out of her throat. "Would you like me to have a word with him?" she asked.

"Nah, he's seen me being charming to you. I can stop now."

"I think 'charming' might be exaggerating a bit. You should probably carry on being nice to me for a while longer."

"We'll see. Seriously though, I'd like it if we could be friends. I feel like a right idiot for what happened that night in Dad's shed. I don't know what came over me. Not that you're not pretty, you're very pretty. I mean, look at you . . . but . . ."

A flush crept across Polly's cheeks. "It's fine," she interrupted. "Of course we can be friends." She wasn't cruel enough to let him carry on tying himself in knots any longer.

"I'm glad," said Mark, looking relieved and rubbing the back of his neck with his hand.

Polly and Mark wolfed down large mugs of coffee and a pile of toast and marmalade before pulling on their welly boots and coats and heading back out to the barn.

It was a beautiful morning with the promise of a little bit of warmth in the air.

All the sheep in the barn seemed to realise it was feeding time and noisily made it quite clear that they expected to be given first priority. Mark quickly whipped around feeding them all except Barbara and her lambs, so Polly could go straight to the back of the shed to check on her favourites. The lambs both stood up as she approached, and she gave them a stroke.

Barbara was lying in the corner still, but her eyes looked brighter and when Mark came over with some fresh hay and placed it by her head, she began chewing contentedly. He checked the ewe over carefully and then showed Polly how to make up the bottles for Bubble and Squeak, and they settled down to feed them both. The lambs were hungry and drank well.

"I'm happy to do the next feed by myself so you can get on," offered Polly as they washed their hands before leaving the barn.

"That would be great. I can go and pick up the formula if you're keeping an eye on them while I'm gone. I don't like to ask Dad in case Barbara goes downhill while I'm out . . ." Mark replied. His sleeves were rolled up and Polly found his arm muscles more than a little distracting.

"I'll stay with them," Polly promised. "They'll be fine."

"Are you sure you've got time though?"

"I'll leave straight after," Polly said, mentally calculating how long it would take her to drive home, get changed and walk to the pub for her after lunch shift.

"Brilliant, thanks," Mark said, his smile making all thoughts of working in the pub fly right out of Polly's head.

* * *

Aunt Sue made her appearance only about ten minutes after Mark left. With everything that had happened, Polly had actually forgotten she was coming.

"Oh, you're here, are you?" she said, as Polly dealt with the gate for her.

"I certainly am," replied Polly. Not even Sue could put her in a bad mood today. "Have you brought the accounts with you?"

"It may have escaped your notice, young lady, but I am a busy woman. I can't be at your beck and call for any little thing."

Polly managed to bite back her retort that as Sue was paid to do the farm's accounts, it was kind of her job to get them to her.

"So you haven't brought them?" Polly asked, fixing a smile on her face.

"I didn't say that now, did I? I've got the tax returns for the last ten years on the back seat, along with all the vets' bills and the electric and phone charges. It took me ages to find them all," Sue said accusingly.

"Thank you," said Polly politely, "but I've got most of that already. There's no need to sort through it, I'm happy to do that." What Polly needed were the details of all the expenditures to do with the farm, there were definitely some discrepancies between what it would cost to look after the animals and what was actually leaving the account as cash but written down as "Hay and Straw" in the ledger John kept to record the farm's day to day expenses, for example. Presumably there were expenses to do with running things which Polly wasn't aware of and so had overlooked in her calculations.

Sue looked extremely put out, "So you don't want this stuff then?"

"I'll have a check through it, there might be something I don't have or is in a clearer form." Polly waited expectantly for Sue to open her car door and hand her the documents.

"I'll need to check with my brother that he's happy for you to have them," said Sue primly.

Polly sighed inwardly, for goodness sake, this woman was ridiculous.

"Well, he's in the house if you'd like to ask him," she said.

"Fine," replied Sue, flouncing off across the yard. Polly couldn't help hoping that she'd step in chicken poo.

Polly decided to go for a little wander to give Sue enough time to complain to John about her, and was pleased when she was joined by Dylan. She suspected he was also trying to avoid a certain someone.

By the time they'd taken a turn of the strawberry fields and come back to check on Barbara and her babies, Sue's car was gone. "She's obviously got more important things to do than hang around here, eh boy?" Polly said, giving Dylan a scratch behind his ear.

Her suspicions were confirmed when she found John and he told her Sue was organising a flower arranging demonstration in the local church hall so couldn't stop for lunch.

"She's left a pile of paperwork for you in the kitchen," John said.

"She doesn't seem very keen on me," Polly admitted.

"Don't you worry about her, duck," he replied kindly. "She'll come round to you."

Polly wasn't convinced, but it would certainly make things easier if John were right.

CHAPTER SEVEN

Polly woke up on Monday morning with a twinge of disappointment that she was in her own bedroom in her own little flat in London. She was due to work in the Bluebell, but not until 5 p.m. — what was she going to do with herself all day she wondered?

She made herself a cup of tea and a couple of slices of toast smothered in butter and jam, which she took back to bed with her. It felt deliciously decadent to return under the covers and enjoy her breakfast while she read her book. Polly guessed there were some benefits to not having a full-time job.

Polly's phone dinged with a WhatsApp message from a number she didn't know. She opened it automatically; it was a photo of Bubble and Squeak. She figured that unless John had suddenly become very tech savvy, it was Mark messaging her. The lambs looked so sweet cuddled up together sleeping and Polly wished she were with them. Her heart longed to be back at Nightingale Farm.

Mark had his plate full already without having to care for two lambs who needed feeding and checking on every few hours on top of everything else. She felt like she should be there, but would Mark even want her around? Would she be in the way? He'd thanked her for helping him the night the twins had been born, but she couldn't very well turn up again less than twenty-four hours after leaving. It wasn't her job to look after the animals and he'd probably think she was interfering.

'Thanks for the photo. How are they doing? Is Barbara any better?' she typed back quickly.

Polly tried to go back to concentrating on her book, but her eyes kept glancing over to the screen, hoping for a reply from Mark. When a message did come through a few minutes later, Polly eagerly snatched up her phone, and was disappointed for the first time in her life to see that it was Alice who'd contacted her.

'Are you free for dinner tomorrow night? I've got someone I'd like you to meet!' said the message.

Polly sighed, she knew a set-up when she saw it.

'A blind date? No thanks!' she sent back.

Almost immediately, her phone started ringing, Alice's name flashing across the screen.

"Hey!" Alice said cheerfully when Polly answered.

"I'm not interested in a blind date. You remember what happened the last time."

"First of all, that was a trick he'd done loads of times! He had no idea it would end with a trip to A&E on this one occasion, and he offered to pay the dry-cleaning bill. And second, you'll really like Seb. He's a freelance surveyor we've been using for ages. Oh, and third, Richard and I will come as well — a double date!"

"It's not that I don't appreciate it Al, but I'm not really in the market for a boyfriend at the moment. I've got enough on my plate with the farm and my shifts at the pub, not to mention looking for a job."

"It's *one* dinner. You have to eat, and you may as well leave your flat to do so. And if you hate him, you don't ever have to see him again. But I know you'll like him!"

Polly sighed. Alice didn't sound like she was going to give up without a fight, and maybe meeting this Seb would help take her mind off Mark. "Alright, fine."

* * *

Polly made an effort for her date the following evening. Alice had sent her a link to Seb's website which had a photo of him on the landing page. She had to admit Seb was handsome. He came complete with broad shoulders, shoulder-length blond hair and blue eyes. She went all out, spending ages on her make-up and treating herself to a new top from Zara during a hurried shopping trip after finishing the early shift at the pub.

The quartet were meeting at 7 p.m. at a Spanish restaurant Alice had heard good things about in Battersea. Polly arrived on time, but she could see everyone else was already seated at a table next to the window. She took the opportunity to sneak a peek at her date: he was just as good-looking, if not more so, as his photograph had suggested. Polly checked her own reflection in the glass door as she pushed it open, smoothing an errant section of hair down at the back of her head.

The group stood to greet Polly as she approached their table. Alice hugged her and whispered, "See, I told you he was gorgeous," into Polly's ear.

"Seb, this is Polly; Polly, Seb," Alice introduced.

"Nice to meet you," said Polly, smiling. She took the seat left for her next to Seb who smiled back at her.

"Shall we get a couple of bottles of Rioja for the table?" suggested Richard.

Everyone agreed and the wine was ordered along with a tapas selection for starters.

The restaurant was warm and welcoming. The food and drink were delicious, and Seb was charming; he was attentive and funny, but Polly wasn't attracted to him. She wished she was, but the plain fact of the matter was that he did nothing for her. Was he too nice? Too friendly? Whatever it was, in this case, the old adage was certainly true: it wasn't him, it was her.

Seb was in the middle of telling a very amusing story about a man selling his house who had been attempting to hide the fact that half the roof was effectively missing, when

Polly heard her mobile ding in her bag. It would be unbelievably rude to check her phone while Seb was in the middle of
his tale, but she was dying to see if she had another message
from Mark.

She waited as patiently as she could until Seb was finished before excusing herself to use the bathroom, taking her
bag with her phone in it with her.

Once she was in the bathroom, she took out her phone,
thrilled to see that the message was indeed from Mark. She
opened it to discover a short video of the lambs snuggled up
together and snoring quietly. It was about the cutest thing
she'd ever seen.

She immediately sent a reply: 'Is Barbara able to feed
Bubble and Squeak now?'

She returned to the table as soon as she'd pressed send,
not wanting anyone to think there was something wrong.

Overall, Polly couldn't have wished for better company.
Seb was lovely and was doing everything he could to entertain her. Alice kept trying to catch Polly's eye — her friend
was so sure that Polly would be over the moon with her date,
and at any other time Polly would have been, but right now
all Polly wanted to do was leave and check her phone, which
had dinged almost as soon as she'd sat back down again.

She made it through the main course, and managed to
smile and laugh appropriately in the right places, though
her heart sank when the others all decided they'd stay for
pudding.

An hour later, and the group were finally standing outside the restaurant ready to leave.

Alice and Richard quickly said their goodbyes — clearly
wanting to leave Polly and Seb on their own together.

"Would you like to go on to a bar?" Seb asked. "I know
a good place only a few minutes' walk from here . . ."

"I'm sorry," she said. She genuinely didn't want to hurt
Seb's feelings. He seemed like a wonderful guy but there was
no point in leading him on. She didn't want to see him again,
even if his hair was impressively shiny. "I've had a really long

day," Polly continued, "and my head is pounding. Would you mind if we called it a night?"

"Of course not!" Seb said, pleasantly. "Can I walk you home or call you a taxi?"

"No, thank you. I'm fine getting home by myself."

Seb leant in and kissed Polly on the cheek.

"May I have your number?" he asked. "I'd love to see you again."

Oh Lord, this was awkward . . . but she needed to be honest.

"I'm sorry, Seb. I'm not sure what Alice has told you, but I'm not looking for a relationship. You see, I lost my job a while ago, and I've got an opportunity I'm trying to make the most of, so, basically, I need to focus on my career at the moment . . ."

She was rambling she knew. This was excruciating.

"Right. Not a problem," he said with a weak smile.

"Well, I guess . . ."

"Yeah, it was good to meet you."

He kissed her on the cheek again before hurrying off.

As soon as Seb was out of sight, Polly whipped out her phone and checked Mark's message.

'The vet says to try her in a few days.'

Polly wished she could be there to see Barbara with her babies, but it wasn't her place, and without an invitation, she didn't feel she could just turn up having only left so recently. And anyway, it sounded like Mark had everything under control, he obviously didn't need her help.

She decided to walk home, after the evening she'd had she could do with the fresh air to clear her head.

But the walk didn't help. The streets were too crowded with people moving between venues or heading home after their evening out. There was too much noise: people talking, music from pubs, cars and buses driving by . . . It was even too bright with all the streetlamps, traffic headlights, and the harsh artificial illumination from shops and office buildings.

She yearned for calm and quiet, for the gentle pace of Nightingale Farm she realised. That was where she wanted to be. Sat next to the Aga with a cup of tea in her hands and Dylan by her feet, or helping with the lambs, or even having another drink of awful cider with Mark. Polly quickened her pace — at least when she was back in her little flat she could relax.

Polly let herself into her building and climbed up the two flights of stairs to her front door.

What was she going to say to Alice? She'd been so excited about setting her up with Seb, Polly didn't want her to be disappointed.

Polly was wondering whether she should just message Alice and admit what had happened. She was saved from making a decision by a text message coming through from her friend.

'How's it going? Isn't Seb great? Call me tomorrow — I want all the dirty details!'

Polly typed out a reply straight away:

'Seb is indeed great — I really should have found out what hair products he uses! But he's not for me — sorry!'

Polly sent her response, and as she anticipated, her mobile started ringing almost immediately.

"Hiya," she said, feeling a wave of affection for her friend, who was always determined in her mission to find Polly a partner. She knew it was kindly meant and only attempted because Alice wanted Polly to be as happy as she was with Richard.

"How could you not like him?!" Alice said without pre-amble. "He's perfect for you! You're not still pining after that Mark guy are you?"

"Maybe a little bit . . ." admitted Polly. "But I think I really do need to focus on work right now, and, to be honest, I wasn't attracted to Seb. I appreciate that sounds stupid given that he was gorgeous and interesting, but it's the truth."

"Well, if you didn't feel a connection, I guess there's no point in forcing it," sighed Alice. "Did you at least let him down gently?"

"He'll be fine," Polly reassured her.

"Alright, well goodnight then, crazy lady! If I didn't have Richard . . ."

Polly laughed and replied, "Goodnight, Alice!" before ending the call. She'd watch the video of the lambs and read Mark's message just once more before she got ready for bed.

* * *

Polly checked her mobile during her break at work on Thursday and a wide grin spread across her face as she saw another WhatsApp message from Mark. When she opened it, she was surprised to find not a photo or video, or even a lamb update, but a request to call him when she was able to.

Polly's stomach fluttered as she pressed the call button, speaking to him on the phone somehow seemed to be a step up in their familiarity with each other. He was probably only wanting to ask her advice on whether to replace an old radiator in one of the cottages or something similarly business related she reminded herself.

"Hi, Polly," Mark said. She hoped she could hear a smile in his voice.

"Hi Mark, I got your message. Is everything alright?"

"Everything's fine, but I've got a big favour to ask."

"Oh yeah?"

"I completely understand if you can't help out, but Dad's been invited to visit his cousin for a couple of days, from tomorrow morning until Sunday evening. I really want him to go because he's been working hard and I think he could do with the break, but I can't manage the night feeds and looking after all the other animals by myself."

"You want me to come and stay at the farm with you?" clarified Polly.

"Even if you could just manage one night? I know it's not exactly in your job description. I could pay you? Out of my own money, not the farm's," he added quickly.

"I wouldn't let you pay me! It'd be my pleasure to help. For both nights," Polly said firmly.

"Thanks, Polly." He sounded relieved. "I appreciate it."

"It's not a problem. I'll come after work tomorrow. I'll be with you by seven," Polly said, feeling horrible that Mark didn't know "work" was her early shift at the Bluebell.

"I'll have supper on," Mark said.

"Great, see you tomorrow then," said Polly before ending the call. She couldn't believe that the grumpy man of just over a mere month ago was requesting her help! She'd been booked to work both Saturday and Sunday to make up for the previous weekend, but she knew it wouldn't be a problem to get someone to cover for her, especially the Sunday shift which was paid at time and a half. She'd simply have to tighten her own purse strings even further for a little while.

* * *

When Polly arrived at the farm the following day, it was already dark. The lights were on in the animal shed, and Mark emerged from it when he heard her approaching the gate so he could open it for her.

"Hey! Where's Dylan?" Polly asked immediately, missing her usual welcome.

"Dad took Dylan with him." Spotting the disappointment on Polly's face, he added, "I know, it's strange without him here."

"Well, I only hope the sheep don't get any weird ideas about stepping out of line with their boss away."

They both chuckled at the thought of Dylan actually doing any of the work he was supposedly trained to do instead of following people around the farm all day in case they needed a lick.

"How's it going?" Polly asked.

"Well, the place hasn't fallen down yet," Mark said with a laugh.

"Glad to hear it."

Polly went straight over to see Bubble and Squeak, who she could hear bleating away from the other end of the shed. She was sure they'd grown in the few days since she'd last seen them in the flesh. She was pleased to see Barbara moving about more.

Mark came to join her. "They're all doing so well. If she'd just had a single birth, Barbara would be able to feed no problem, but she still needs a bit of help with the two of them."

"I can't believe the difference in them all after less than a week."

"It's amazing, isn't it?" Mark said, watching the animals with real pride in his eyes. "And because they've been handled such a lot by us since birth, they'll be perfect for the petting zoo. I've got a few things to finish off, food'll be ready in about half an hour."

"Let me give you a hand," Polly offered, and she was soon knee-deep in straw and goodness only knows what else as she cleaned out one of the stalls while Mark brought in the animals who'd spent the day outside.

Once all the animals had been taken care of, they washed their hands in the freezing water from the sink by the shed door.

"Sorry there's no towel, it must be in the wash," apologised Mark.

"No worries," Polly replied, wiping her hands on her jeans.

Dylan's absence was definitely felt when they made their way into the warm kitchen, but Polly consoled herself with the thought that the dog would be having a lovely time with John.

The kitchen smelt delicious. "What's cooking?" Polly asked.

"Fish pie," Mark replied. "But I can't take credit for it, Dad made an extra one a while ago and popped it in the freezer, I'm just heating it up."

"Can I do anything to help?"

"Could you lay the table? I'll get the peas on. It should all be done in a couple of minutes."

They shuffled around each other. Polly tried to think of something to say. It was weird without John chattering away about the garden while Dylan snored by the Aga. She and Mark had already caught up about the farm and the lambs, what else did they have to talk about? Work was the first thing that came to Polly's mind, but she definitely needed to pre-empt him questioning her about her own job.

His carpentry was safe territory Polly realised, and she was interested to know more about it.

"Have you been able to do much carpentry for your business?" she asked as Mark plated up.

"It's had to be sidelined as we've been focusing on the farm, but I've been able to fit a bit in, and I want to be able to build it up properly again once the farm is up and running."

"How did you get started in it?" she asked, genuinely curious.

"I spent years trying to figure out what I wanted to do — I actually studied accountancy at university, but hated it. I kept coming back to carpentry, which I used to do with my grandfather when I was little, so I did an apprenticeship part-time while working as an accountant. When Mum inherited the farm I think she would have liked me to come and help with it, but she understood that I'd only recently got my studio in Brighton and was finally able to make enough money that I could be a carpenter full-time. I was never going to make millions, but I was happy."

Mark turned and placed their two loaded plates on the table before continuing.

"When I found out Mum was ill, I offered to move back, but she wouldn't hear of it, and then she deteriorated so quickly . . . Mum and I were very close, and I think I shut everyone out after she died, even Dad to a certain extent. It was my business that kept me going."

"It must have been a really rough time," Polly said, putting her hand on his to comfort him instinctively. A tiny burst of electricity shot through her and she looked at Mark to gauge his reaction. He didn't meet her gaze, but he also didn't move his own hand away.

"It was," he murmured, "and I found it so painful to see the farm without Mum there. It made the loss worse somehow."

"How do you feel about it now?"

"I still miss Mum, of course I do, but I'm glad I'm helping Dad and that we're building the farm back up again. I think Mum would be proud."

"I'm sure she would be."

They settled down opposite each other with their food.

"Something I really need to get sorted out for my business is a website," Mark continued, in a lighter tone. "When I had my workshop in Brighton I pretty much relied on word of mouth, and there were a couple of shops which stocked my smaller items. I'm not quite starting from nothing again here, but I need people to be able to find out how to buy from me again, and a way for new customers to see some of what I have to offer."

"I can help you with that if you like," offered Polly.

"That would be brilliant, if you're sure you have time; I'm useless with that kind of stuff. I've always been better with my hands . . ." He stopped abruptly. "I mean . . ."

"It's okay," said Polly, struggling to suppress her laughter at his very sweet discomfort. "I know what you mean. I'm the opposite, I've always been rubbish with my hands. It won't take long at all to get you a website using one of the easy build sites. How fancy do you want it?"

"Not fancy at all!" admitted Mark. "It doesn't need more than a landing page with my contact details and some photos of my work I guess."

"Have you got photos?" Polly asked in between bites.

"A few, I'm not sure they're very professional though."

"That's alright." Polly quickly checked the weather app on her mobile. "It looks like it's going to be a gorgeous day tomorrow, perfect for a photo shoot if we have time."

Once they had finished eating and clearing up, Polly got her laptop out and began work on Mark's website. Mark sent her over photos of his work from his phone and his own computer. There were a couple that were good enough quality, but they'd definitely need to take some more in decent light.

They worked quietly together, passing things back and forth, only stopping briefly when Mark left to feed Bubble and Squeak.

"Are you sure you're happy with me bossing you about like this?" asked Polly at one point.

"Quite happy. It would have taken me forever to have sorted this out by myself, and who knows when I'd actually have got round to it."

Mark stifled a yawn.

"I'm sorry," Polly said immediately. "I'm keeping you up."

"No, I'm sorry. This is great, but maybe we could continue tomorrow? If the lambs have a quick feed now, I'll get a couple of hours' sleep in before they need to be seen to again."

"I can go out and see to Bubble and Squeak now," Polly offered. "I know what to do and I'm supposed to be here to help you with them."

"That would actually be great, thanks."

Polly checked her watch. "So, it's ten now. If you do the feed at one, I'll sort them out at four."

"And I'll get to them at seven," finished Mark. "That would be a huge help. Are you sure you're okay out there in the dark by yourself?"

"Of course I am," scoffed Polly.

"Even though Dylan won't be there to keep you company?"

"You forget, I'm the woman who made it through the night in an abandoned cottage without any heating or electricity. I'm pretty tough."

"How could I forget?" replied Mark. "Well, if you do run into any problems, just come and wake me up."

Mark went upstairs to bed and Polly put on her shoes, coat and a hat. She took a big torch which was kept by the back door. Polly was determined to get on with the job at hand and not worry about the dark as she gingerly made her way across the yard to the barn. The torch's beam illuminated the yard, but it was hard to keep it steady as she was also carrying the two made up bottles of formula for the lambs.

Thankfully, the barn was much warmer than outside. It was peaceful with the animals snuffling around. Polly went into Barbara's stall and was greeted by Bubble and Squeak, who clearly anticipated she was bringing food.

Without knowing exactly how much milk the twins were getting from their mother, the idea was to use the bottles to top them up so they'd definitely be having all they needed. Polly sat on a hay bale Mark had put in the corner of the stall. She had no trouble encouraging the lambs to come and feed, it was getting them to take turns that was the problem. In the end she gave up and attempted to feed them simultaneously, a bottle in each hand. The results were mixed, but the lambs seemed happy and that was the important thing.

Once they'd finished, Polly slipped back into the silent house and up to her room, doing her very best not to disturb Mark. She heard Mark get up at one, but was in a deep sleep when her own alarm went off at four. The last thing she wanted to do was get out of her warm bed and go out into the cold night, but a promise was a promise, and she wouldn't let the lambs go hungry. Groggily, she climbed out of bed and went downstairs. Mark had left a note for her:

"Hope you're not regretting your offer! I'll make you a bacon butty for (late) breakfast as a thank you."

Polly smiled to herself, all of a sudden, she didn't mind being up early nearly as much as she had.

* * *

Polly slept in until 9 a.m. She was still tired, but she could hear Mark moving around in the kitchen and she knew there would be plenty to do around the farm.

She had a quick shower and got dressed. Bacon was sizzling away on the Aga by the time she made her way downstairs.

"Good morning," said Mark cheerfully. "I heard the shower going so figured it was safe to get the bacon started. I'm starving."

"Me too," admitted Polly. "How are the lambs this morning?"

"Hungry!" Mark replied. "Hopefully only a few more nights of this though, Barbara's coming along really well."

They ate their breakfast and went outside so Polly could give Mark a hand finishing off the farm chores.

"So are there actual nightingales on the farm? That might attract some more visitors. I could add it to the website if there are," suggested Polly as they hauled hay up to the cows in the pasture. The grass wasn't quite plentiful enough for them to do without it.

"We do have a few," answered Mark. "They migrate and they'll be back around Easter. I'd rather you didn't draw attention to them though. There aren't nearly as many nightingales here as there used to be, numbers have dropped all over the country and Kent is one of their last strongholds apparently. They nest on the ground, usually on this side of the copse over there and I don't want them disturbed by overenthusiastic tourists traipsing around up there."

"No problem, I won't mention them," said Polly. "We'll leave them in peace."

The clouds cleared as the morning went on, and after a quick lunch, they went to Mark's workshop and began carrying out some of his favourite pieces. He polished them with beeswax while Polly arranged them for the photographs, and then she began snapping away.

"Do you have a photo of yourself we could use?" she asked once she'd taken all the pictures she needed of the furniture.

Mark screwed up his face, "You don't need a photo of me, no one wants to see that."

"I'm afraid they do," said Polly with a shrug. "People like to 'meet the maker'. You must have one decent picture we can use."

Mark looked embarrassed. "I don't tend to take photos of myself."

"Alright," said Polly. "Stand over there by the chest of drawers, and give me your best smile."

Mark did as instructed. He positioned himself somewhat awkwardly, leaning against the furniture and turned his mouth slowly into a grimace.

Polly fought to hide her amusement. "Maybe if you tried to relax a little bit . . ."

"I hate having my photo taken," Mark mumbled.

How can someone so good-looking be so self-conscious in front of a camera? Polly wondered to herself.

"Try pretending the camera isn't there. Let's just continue chatting like we were," she suggested.

"Okay," mumbled Mark, barely moving his lips.

Silence ensued.

"So . . ." said Polly, breaking the stalemate. "Once we get the furniture back inside, I can upload the photos on your website and put the final touches to the wording. Then the site can go live."

"That would be great," Mark replied, his face relaxing into a smile and his eyes meeting hers. Polly's stomach flipped, but she somehow remembered to press the button on her phone to take a burst of photographs.

CHAPTER EIGHT

Happily, Mark continued to send Polly regular updates on Bubble and Squeak every couple of days after she'd returned home. They'd begun feeding from their mother exclusively, and Barbara was proving to be a very good mum. The weather was warming up nicely, and they were spending lots of time outside — they seemed to enjoy following Mark around and getting in his way while he got his jobs done. They weren't allowed in his workshop though.

Polly's job hunting still hadn't led to anything. She'd broadened the search of what she was applying for and was sending off her CV and filling out plenty of applications, but was getting nowhere. She knew she couldn't carry on withholding the truth from her family for much longer, and was in the process of trying to get up the courage to come clean. Could she get it over and done with over the phone, or had it been going on for so long, that it really ought to be admitted face-to-face?

In better news, the land auction had gone really well, the money raised would pay for the renovation of the cottages and everything needed to set up the camping field.

Polly had been working hard behind the scenes — her photos of John's hedges had been great publicity for the farm's opening weekend — she'd managed to get them in the local paper and a couple of magazines. The farm now had a working website and a Facebook page, complete with plenty of photos of Bubble and Squeak of course. Mark's new website had also been linked to the farm's Facebook page. The photos Polly had taken had turned out really well, so well that she couldn't seem to stop clicking on them. It was puzzling how drawn she felt to Mark. She was glad he'd thawed to her, it made her job much easier, but it wasn't just that. He was so self-contained, but he really loved his dad and was trying so hard to turn the fortunes of the farm around. He was also strong and completely trustworthy Polly was sure — which was one of the reasons why she felt so guilty about not being truthful about her circumstances.

Polly was about to run out of the door to another shift at the Bluebell when she received a phone call from John asking her to visit on Easter Sunday — the first day the farm would be open to the public. Maggie would be selling tea, coffee and cake, John was busy harvesting rhubarb, spring onions, asparagus, spring cabbages, and purple sprouting broccoli to sell. They had an Easter egg hunt planned, and plenty of little chicks to delight visiting children. Mark and John had also taken Polly's advice and had acquired more animals from a rescue centre she'd recommended, including four pygmy goats to add to what would be their petting zoo. The play area wasn't completed yet, but the new nature trail was, and John would be giving tractor rides around the farm, which would allow visitors to see everything else that would be ready over the next few months.

Of course, Polly said she'd be there. As soon as she was off the phone, she messaged Alice to see if she and Richard would like to come too. She really wanted her best friend to meet John and see the farm, and also, she had to admit, give her opinion on Mark.

Now all the weekend needed was good weather. Maggie's food would be served inside, and one of the smaller outhouses had been converted into a little farm shop so the veg would be safe from a downpour, and the animals all had stalls inside the large animal shed now, but they were very unlikely to have many visitors willing to drive out to them if it was pouring with rain.

Thankfully the forecast remained good and Polly woke up on Easter Sunday morning delighted to see it was bright and sunny outside. There would even be a little warmth to the sun later in the day — they couldn't have asked for better.

Polly decided to stick with wearing her trusty wellies as she wasn't sure how muddy some of the nature trail might be, but teamed them with her favourite skinny jeans and a pale grey fitted shirt. She knew enough about the farm and its inhabitants by now to pack a change of clothes in her car.

The traffic getting out of London was worse than she'd anticipated, and so Polly was later arriving than she'd planned on being. By the time she pulled into the open farm gate, she was thrilled to see there were already visitors. In fact, the small area set aside as a car park was looking rather full. She managed to squeeze her little car into one of the few remaining spaces.

She spotted Mark straight away and headed over to him.

"Hey," he beamed. "Glad you could make it."

"I wouldn't have missed it for the world," answered Polly. "I'm so glad so many people are coming, thank goodness you've got decent weather."

"Yes." He glanced around. "I think I'm going to need to set up a second car park."

"Where's Dylan?" she asked, missing her usual welcome.

"He's with Dad for the day, he loves a ride in the tractor."

She laughed. "Can I do anything to help?"

Mark gave her a grateful smile. "Could you wander around and keep an eye on things? Dad's just started the tractor rides, and Maggie's manning her café and is taking the money from the farm shop. Aunt Sue should be here in a bit, but I'm going to be stuck dealing with the parking for a while. We've got a local couple, Tash and Clive, helping out with the petting zoo."

"Of course, not a problem," replied Polly, turning to leave.

"Oh, and there's an official Nightingale Farm top for you in the kitchen," Mark called out, a grin escaping as he did so.

"An official top?"

"Oh, yes!"

Polly dutifully hurried into the house where she found a neatly folded logoed navy blue polo shirt waiting for her on the kitchen table. She quickly changed in the bathroom and went back outside to see what she could do to help.

More people were arriving. Polly signalled to Mark that she'd head into the animal barn. He gave her a thumbs up.

The space looked very different to the first time she'd seen it: it was warm and bright, and smelt of clean straw. All the stalls had been repaired and painted. On the door to each stall was a wooden sign with an engraving of the type of animal the stall contained and their name. The carving was beautiful, Mark's handiwork was everywhere.

Families were milling around, looking in the stalls. At the far end of the barn was a large area surrounded by a low fence. The couple Mark had mentioned were in there along with a selection of animals that children could stroke and ask questions about.

Polly quickly hunted out Barbara's stall and was amazed to see how big Bubble and Squeak had become — she could hardly believe they were the same lambs. They were so inquisitive and came straight over to her. She really hoped she'd get to have a cuddle with them when things were less busy afterwards.

She went around the rest of the area, there were four more sheep, some chickens, a family of potbellied pigs, and some gorgeous donkeys and super fluffy, grey rabbits.

Everything seemed to be running smoothly and all the visitors were having a good time. A large sign by the barn's back door directed her to the duck pond and "Goat Parkour".

As keen as Polly was to meet the ducks, how could she resist the lure of "Goat Parkour"?

The goat paddock had a large sign on the gate with the goats' names on, and some information about them and how they'd been adopted from a local rescue centre. Polly made sure she took plenty of photos to use for social media and other publicity.

The goats had shelters with steps and slopes for them to use to climb up onto the low roofs. There were also a variety of tree stumps and seesaws for them to balance on. It was a proper goat adventure playground. At 3 p.m. there was a chance for visitors to feed them, which Polly suspected would be very popular.

The goats were very entertaining. Alternatively chasing each other like crazy, noisily coming to check out onlookers, and clambering up and down their various pieces of "parkour" equipment.

The duck pond which Polly visited next was small, but charming, with a family of ducks including five ducklings who followed their mother around loyally when they weren't splashing around chasing one another or playing hide and seek in the reeds at the edge of the water.

Next Polly followed the signposted circular nature walk which took her past the ponies in their paddock. She stopped to stroke their noses and made a mental note to speak to John about the possibility of pony rides in the future. They'd touched on it briefly before and had agreed it would be complicated — they'd need an instructor and insurance for starters, but it was definitely worth considering.

Polly was impressed by how well organised the day was — John and Mark had thought everything out and it already looked like it was a big success.

As she completed her tour and returned to the farmyard, she spotted John approaching in his tractor. The trailer it pulled contained lots of smiling children. He drove into the farmyard and stopped in front of the barn, waving. Dylan gave her a friendly "woof" when he saw her. Polly walked over and lent a hand getting everyone out.

"Have you had a chance to wander around?" John asked excitedly once the trailer was empty.

"I have. It looks brilliant!" said Polly, honestly. "I can't believe how much you've managed to do."

"It's been hard work," John admitted. "But it's been worth it."

"Can I do anything to help?"

John sighed gratefully. "A cup of coffee would be lovely."

"I'll be right back with it," Polly said, turning towards the farmhouse.

"Actually," said John, looking sheepish, "could I have one from Maggie's café, please? It's over there." He pointed towards the building that used to be the dairy and which had a steady stream of people coming and going.

"Of course," said Polly, doing her best to hide the smile threatening to escape her lips. "I hadn't had a chance to check it out yet."

* * *

Maggie's café was still a little rough and ready, but her bright smile and delicious-looking food made it feel welcoming. A long trestle table had been set up and she had a counter along the back wall with a kettle and a coffee machine. A few tables with bright-checked tablecloths partnered with cutely mismatched wooden chairs were set up, most of which Polly guessed were from Mark's workshop. A door led through to the farm shop so it was easy for customers to bring anything they wanted to purchase to Maggie, and then get lured into buying a slice of cake as well.

Maggie finished serving a customer and came round the counter to give Polly a warm hug when Polly introduced herself.

"It's so good to meet you finally, John's told me so much about you! What can I get you? On the house!" she asked.

"Oh, thank you!" Polly replied. "I came to get a coffee for John, but I'd love one too."

"Americano, like John? Or can I tempt you with a gingerbread latte or a cappuccino?"

"Wow, a gingerbread latte sounds amazing."

"And you must have a cake, what'll it be?"

Polly looked over the assortment of goodies. The cakes looked delicious displayed on tiered stands. Sticky maple syrup flapjacks vied for space with rich chocolate and raspberry brownies and muffins full of fat, juicy blueberries. An imposing Victoria sponge and a vivid red velvet cake were cut into thick slices. The only item a little out of place was a rather sad little floral plate of thin scones at the back of the counter. The scones were split and filled with what looked suspiciously like margarine combined with the thinnest layer of jam imaginable. Polly wondered what the story was behind them.

"I'll have a slice of the red velvet, please," Polly said, drawn back to the more appetising options. "It looks wonderful."

"I hope you like it. Would you take a treat for John to go with his coffee?"

"Sure, what do you think he'd like?" asked Polly.

"His favourite are the flapjacks," Maggie said, and went to pick one up with her tongs.

"John will want one of my homemade scones. They've always been his favourite," said a loud, indignant voice.

Polly turned around and found herself face-to-face with Aunt Sue.

Maggie just smiled, placed the flapjack back down and put a scone on the plate for John instead.

"It doesn't look like you've sold many of them," Sue continued, huffily. "You need to move them closer to the front so people can see them properly."

"Good idea," said Maggie, brightly, and she swapped Sue's scones with her brownies.

"I'm guessing you're who I should give the receipt for the scone ingredients to? I expect to be reimbursed," Sue said, thrusting a supermarket receipt into Polly's hand.

"Um, sure," said Polly, glancing at the receipt for £8.37, including organic butter and strawberry conserve, neither of which she was convinced had been used for the scones. "I'll transfer the money into your bank account."

"See that you do, I am a pensioner you know."

Aunt Sue stomped off without waiting for a response, presumably to go and find something else to complain about.

Polly and Maggie shared an amused look as Maggie added a flapjack onto John's plate and placed it on a tray with his drink.

There was a lull in customers so Maggie suggested that she take John's drink and snack to him.

"You have a sit down behind the counter in case anyone comes in. The prices are all on the chalkboard and I'll only be a minute," Maggie said.

Polly settled down with her cake and coffee and Maggie hurried off, holding the tray in one hand and tidying her hair with the other.

Almost as soon as Maggie stepped out of the café, a family of four came in. Thankfully they only wanted cold drinks from the little fridge Maggie had under the counter, but Polly was very pleased to see Maggie return at the same time as another group of visitors arrived. Maggie looked a little flushed and there was a definite extra spring to her step.

Polly hung around with her for a while having a chat about Maggie's plans for the café and helping to serve all the hungry visitors who wandered in.

She really liked Maggie. She was so friendly, kind, and easy to talk to. She couldn't help but compare her to prickly Aunt Sue who was awkward and unfriendly even though Polly had done her best to be nice to her.

An hour into helping in the makeshift café, Polly felt a tap on her shoulder. She turned around and came face-to-face with Alice.

"Hey you!" Polly said, happily. "You made it!" She hugged her friend and Richard before introducing them to Maggie. "Maggie, this is my friend, Alice, and her partner, Richard."

"Lovely to meet you," said Maggie, brightly.

Some more customers came in, so Polly and her entourage moved out of the way to allow Maggie to serve them.

"So, we met Mark!" said Alice, as soon as they were out of Maggie's earshot. Before Polly could comment, her friend added, "How could you ever have thought he was grumpy? He was really friendly! And so handsome!"

Richard cleared his throat noisily.

"Not as handsome as Richard, obviously," said Alice, quickly, grinning. "But, Pol, I need to warn you: I saw your sister's people carrier pulling into the gate just before I came in here."

"What?!" said Polly, panic-stricken. What on earth was her sister doing here? How did she even know about the farm?

"Is everything alright, Polly?" asked Maggie, who'd come over to join them.

"Yes!" replied Polly, as cheerfully as she could manage. "Apparently my sister, Julie, is here."

"Your sister?" said Maggie, "How nice of her to come to support you! I can't wait to meet her."

Polly forced a smile, her mind racing as to how she was going to deal with this situation: her sister still thought she was employed by her old company, and Polly didn't want her bringing anything up about her work in front of John or Mark which might lead to her having to directly lie to them. She needed to intercept her sister before she had a chance to talk to anyone.

"I'll go track her down," said Polly, brightly. "Alice? Richard? You coming?" Her eyes beseeched her friends to join her in her quest.

"Sure," Alice replied, immediately, and took Richard firmly by the hand.

They hurried out of the café.

Julie's people carrier was indeed in the car park.

"Where do you think she'll head first?" Alice asked, looking around.

"She'll have Michael and Olivia with her," Polly thought out loud. "Olivia loves pigs, so I bet they'll start by visiting them."

Sure enough, there was Julie, looking like a Boden catalogue had exploded over her, with Michael and Olivia fussing over the piglets. But things were even worse than Polly had anticipated: Julie's hedge fund manager husband, Phil, was unusually with them — he typically worked most weekends, and was dressed in his usual office attire minus the tie — and. . . so were Polly's mum, Ruth, and dad, Arthur.

Polly wasn't sufficiently prepared to meet them all when they turned as one to move on to the next animals and spotted her.

"Auntie Polly!" called out the children, excitedly. They ran over to her, hugging her tightly.

"What are you guys doing here?" Polly asked as she ruffled their hair.

"We came to see the animals and to surprise you!" explained six-year-old Olivia, who was dressed as Pippi Longstocking it seemed, complete with long pigtails.

"Mummy said she wanted to find out what you'd been up to," added Michael, a curly-haired child who proved there was no point in putting a four-year-old in smart chinos and a button-down shirt when they're going to visit a farm.

Polly couldn't help laughing, especially when she saw her older sister's indignant, slightly abashed face at being caught out. "Hi Julie," she managed. "Good to see you, Phil. And Mum and Dad. This really is a whole family outing!"

Julie answered for her group as a whole, "Well, Mum bumped into the chap who runs this place at a farmers' market last weekend — he had a stall there — what's his name again?" she asked, turning to her mother for assistance.

"John," Ruth and Polly answered at the same time.

"Anyway," continued Julie, "He said they were opening to the public today, and that you'd been helping him, like Mum suggested."

"He said there's no way he could have done it without you," continued Ruth, proudly. "According to him, they most probably would have lost the farm by now if you hadn't stepped in to help out."

Polly primarily felt embarrassment at being the centre of attention, but she was also touched that John would say those things, and at her mother's reaction to them. That didn't change the fact though that her family still didn't know that she'd lost her job months ago, and neither did John or Mark, and now would be a very bad time for them all to find out. What a scene that would cause. How hurt John would be, and she hated to think of him and Mark not trusting her. Of course, they might also think that, as she was made redundant from her last job, she wasn't capable of what she said she was, and would therefore be unhappy with her continuing to work with them because of that as much as her dishonesty.

What a mess she'd got herself into! She wished she'd just bitten the bullet and told the truth straight away, but it was all very well to say that now, wasn't it? And, perhaps if she had, she wouldn't be here, her family's interference might have led her in another direction. . .

She was dragged from her contemplation by a little hand pulling on her arm to get her attention: Olivia wanted to show her the piglets and to discuss the possibility of her getting one for her next birthday.

Polly wandered around the farm again with her friends and family and, to her own surprise, found she was enjoying herself. She'd missed seeing her little niece and nephew during her period of self-enforced isolation from them, and everyone was in good spirits. Even her sister's endless setting up of her children in cute poses for Instagram photos failed to annoy her, especially as Polly was hoping she could swipe some of the best ones for the farm's promotional materials.

She saw Mark checking on the goats, and quickly tried to lead her group in the opposite direction and out of sight along the nature trail, but he spotted her and walked over to them.

"Hey," he said. "I thought I'd come over and find out what you think of the place so far. I know it's not perfect yet . . ."

"It's brilliant," said Polly, quickly. Noticing her family all looking at her expectantly, she said, "Mark, I know you've already met my friends, Alice and Richard, and this is my family who drove over to have a peek at what you've been up to."

"What *we've* been up to," corrected Mark, putting his arm around Polly's shoulder, sending an unanticipated electric jolt through her. "We'd still be in such a mess if it wasn't for you and all your hard work."

Polly blushed and pointed out the first of the trail signs to the children in an attempt to move the subject away from her and how much time she'd devoted to Nightingale Farm in the last couple of months. Time she couldn't possibly have spent if she'd still been working full-time as her family believed.

Thankfully Polly's tactic worked and everyone began walking along the trail, enjoying pointing out the little, half-hidden, wooden animal sculptures along the way.

"Will you have time to hang around after everyone's left so we can go through how the day's gone?" Mark asked, quietly, gazing at her intently.

"Sure," replied Polly, immediately, meeting his eye and, for some reason, blushing.

"Great, see you later then," he said with a smile, and set off back towards the animal shed, leaving Polly to catch up with her group.

Alice immediately took her best friend aside as she rejoined them. "Mark my words, young lady," she whispered, "I'm foreseeing more kissing in the future between you too." Polly opened her mouth to protest, but her friend just repeated, "Mark my words."

CHAPTER NINE

"Wow!" commented Mark, closing the farm gate as the last of the visitors drove off. "What a day!"

"I can't believe how busy it was! There didn't seem to be a lull at all," Polly said.

All her friends and family had left a while ago, her mother rather put out that Polly didn't depart with them and go back to her parents' house for supper, but, aside from the fact that the more time she spent with her family the guiltier she felt about lying to them, she'd told Mark she'd hang around and didn't want to break her word.

Polly had to admit that, as crazy as they drove her, it had been good to see her family. She'd promised to take her niece and nephew to the cinema and for burgers afterwards the following month, which she hoped would make up, at least a little bit, for her recent neglect of them.

And she had decided she would finally tell her family the truth about her job. She should have done it months before and things were only going to get worse and more complicated the longer the deception went on. Presumably that also meant she'd need to come clean to John and Mark, but she hadn't hashed out the logistics of that yet.

"I think I've definitely earned a drink," decided Mark. "Will you join me?"

"As long as it's not cider." She laughed.

"I think I can promise no cider."

A look passed between them. Such a lot had changed since the night of their kiss, it seemed to Polly like they were two different people back then — certainly they now held much changed opinions of one another.

John's tractor pulled into the yard as Polly and Mark began walking to the farmhouse so they waited for him to climb down and join them.

Polly could see John was tired, which was hardly surprising, it had been a long day. Not wanting to embarrass him by offering her arm, she contented herself with staying close to him in case he needed her as they went into the house. Mark had obviously had the same idea, which led to a comical moment when they all reached the front door at the same moment.

Guessing what they were up to, John said, "Don't you two fuss, I'm fine. Just need a sit down. I've had a wonderful day."

"Are you sure there's nothing I can do?" Polly asked.

"Actually," said John, "Could you see if Maggie's alright and if she needs a hand with anything? Do you think she'd like to stay for supper? She must be exhausted."

"I'm sure she'd love to," said Polly. "I'll check on her and then I'll be right back."

She headed over to the café where Maggie was finishing cleaning up. Everything looked spick and span, and Polly could see how lovely the space would be when it was finished. All that remained of the many goodies Maggie had had for sale was the sad little collection of scones made by Aunt Sue.

"What should I do with these?" Maggie asked. "Do you think Sue will want them back?"

"She'll just be cross they didn't sell," said Polly. Then a bolt of inspiration hit her: "Let's feed them to the pigs! They'll destroy the evidence in seconds!"

Giggling like a couple of naughty schoolgirls, Polly and Maggie hurried over to the animal shed as quickly and quietly as they could, checking over their shoulders frequently in case Aunt Sue should somehow appear out of thin air and catch them in the act.

Polly emptied the contents of the plate into the pig pen. The pigs came trotting over to the scones, gave them a thorough sniffing and seemed reluctant to tuck in. After a moment or so, some of them even began to wander off in search of something more interesting.

Maggie looked horrified. "They're not going to eat them, are they?" she whispered as she looked frantically around her for a solution.

A couple of the piglets continued to sniff suspiciously at the food, but Polly couldn't help but agree that it didn't look like there was much hope. She racked her brain frantically for a plan; what could they do? She thought pigs ate anything. Surely Aunt Sue's baking couldn't be that bad.

"I guess I'll have to go in and retrieve them," Polly declared heroically. She wasn't too sure about pigs if she was to be completely honest. Particularly being in the pen with them. They were quite large after all . . . "We'll get rid of them somewhere else."

She nervously began to undo the latch on the gate, and the huge mother pig chose that moment to stand up. Polly hesitated. That was a really big pig. The sow, as if sensing what Polly was about to do, laboriously trundled over to the abandoned scones, and in about ten seconds flat, had wolfed down the lot.

"Thank goodness for that," sighed Maggie, gratefully.

They looked at each other and grinned.

"Now that's over with," Polly said, "John wanted to know if you'd like to join the rest of us for some supper at the farmhouse."

"That would be so nice," said Maggie, then she looked anxious. "But I must look a terrible mess."

"You look absolutely lovely," said Polly. "Please come."

"Alright, I shall."

The pair returned to the café and locked up before wandering back over to the farmhouse.

John was ensconced in his favourite armchair in the sitting room close to the wood burner. He was pleased to see Polly and Maggie arrive. "Mark's having a shower," he explained. "He'll be back down in a minute. Didn't it go well?"

"Brilliantly! I practically sold out!" Maggie said, happily. She settled down in the chair next to John's.

"Would you pop the CD player on for us please, Polly?"

"Of course." Polly walked across the room and turned on the machine. A Manic Street Preachers album started up — John was pretty cool.

Mark chose this moment to come down the stone staircase next to her. He was fresh out of the shower. His dark hair was damp and he smelt delicious.

"Do you want to give me a hand cooking?" he asked Polly.

"Sure. What are we having?"

"Your guess is as good as mine at the moment," replied Mark, laughing. "We'll have to have a root around the cupboards."

"I'm sure we can come up with something."

"Can I get you a celebratory glass of wine?"

She smiled. "Absolutely."

"Dad? Maggie?"

"A beer for me, son," replied John.

"Wine would be lovely," Maggie said.

Mark began getting drinks together while Polly did her best to come up with some cooking inspiration from the cupboards.

"How about pizza?" she suggested. "You've got plenty of flour to make the dough, tinned tomatoes, cheese, and we'll use whatever else we can rustle together as other toppings."

"Pizza sounds like a fantastic idea."

"Do you need any help in there?" called out Maggie.

"You relax, we'll be fine," Polly called back.

Once she and Mark were out of John's hearing, Mark turned to Polly and quietly asked, "Do you think Dad's okay? He was a really funny colour when he was coming into the house, and I caught him holding his chest at one point."

"I think he's very tired," Polly said honestly. "It's been a long day for both of you, and it must be quite emotional for him as well. He seems happy and comfortable now, and we can keep a close eye on him for the rest of the evening."

Mark nodded in agreement, Polly's words seemed to relax him, at least a little.

Polly and Mark got to work. She made the dough while he dealt with toppings and tomato sauce. They were never going to be traditionally Italian, but Polly's cheat base, taught to her by her mum years ago of self-raising flour, olive oil, salt and water, came together quickly and would work well with the cheddar, a large block of which was the only cheese in the fridge. Peppers, onions and mushrooms were sliced up and soon the pizzas were being loaded into the oven.

The heat from the Aga combined with the scrummy food smells, the music drifting through from the next room, and the wine, created a very welcoming atmosphere.

Polly threw together a salad as Mark cleared and laid the kitchen table, and it wasn't long before they were serving up.

John and Maggie came through and made sure every-one's glasses were refilled, and they settled down to their meal.

"This is delicious," commented Maggie. "What a treat. Thank you both."

"Glad you like it," Polly replied, pleased everyone was enjoying the food.

"Polly, has Mark mentioned he'll be staying overnight in London next week?" asked John.

"No, he hasn't," Polly said, glancing at Mark.

"There's a carpentry fair thing I go to every year," Mark explained. "It runs over a couple of days, I booked my ticket last year and can't get a refund. I've been thinking about putting some feelers out to see if anyone would like to buy it off me, but I've probably left it too late now."

"Don't be daft, son," said John immediately. "You've got to go. You paid for that ticket months ago, using your own money, and you look forward to it every year."

"Yeah, but then there's the cost of booking a hotel room as well," Mark argued.

"Why don't you just stay the night at mine?" Polly found herself suggesting before her brain could catch up with her mouth. "It's only small, but you're more than welcome to my sofa. I'm told it's very comfy."

"Are you sure?" Mark asked, looking at her.

Polly wasn't completely certain if she was, but she couldn't very well take back her offer now. "Absolutely," she replied. "The tube station's close by, you can leave your car outside my flat and use public transport to get to the fair."

"That's all sorted then," said John, contentedly taking another bite of his pizza.

Polly's gaze met Mark's over the table. Was it just her imagination, or did he look as nervous as she felt?

* * *

A few days later, and Polly was making the final preparations before Mark arrived to stay at her flat. Why had she even invited him, she asked herself grumpily. A cheap hotel wouldn't have cost him a lot, and maybe he would have preferred that but felt obliged to take up her offer. Didn't he know anyone else in London he could have crashed with? It was only for one night after all. Did she feel she owed him because she'd stayed at the farm?

Her flat was tiny, but it had still taken her a long time to clean it all thoroughly for her guest. She'd even had to change her shifts at the pub to fit around him visiting. She'd got back from work an hour before, and she'd been putting the finishing touches to herself and her flat ever since.

The butterflies in her stomach went into overdrive as she heard the shrill ring of her intercom: there was no turning back now. She pressed the button, "I'm coming," she said and hurried down the stairs to the building's communal front door.

Mark looked completely out of place on the doorstep, uprooted from his country life which was all Polly had ever seen him in. He carried a bottle of Chablis and a bunch of gladioli and had his rucksack containing his overnight things slung over his shoulder, which struck Polly as rather sweet. She could imagine him as a little boy coming home from school.

"Hey," she said, shyly.

"Hey," Mark responded, then added, "These are for you," and handed over the wine and flowers.

"Thank you," replied Polly, standing back to let him in. "Come this way, my flat's on the second floor."

They walked up the stairs, Polly intensely aware of Mark close behind her. "Was the fair good?" she asked as she let him into her home.

"Yeah, it was. I met some interesting people, and may have a couple of commissions booked," said Mark, following her into the kitchen. "Though I don't find it easy to make small talk for hours on end."

"I can definitely see that about you," said Polly, teasingly.

Mark looked around, taking everything in it seemed.

"I like your flat, you've got amazing views," he commented, politely. "Have you lived here long?"

"A couple of years. When I first moved to London, I stayed in the most awful bedsit. There was one bathroom between six of us, and it was gross. Everyone else living there was Australian and were travelling together. Then all four of the guys got girlfriends, who basically moved in as well, so there was no hope of ever finding the shower free or any room for your food in the fridge."

"Sounds fun."

"It felt so luxurious to have space for myself when I found this place, even though it's hardly huge."

Mark laughed.

"What would you like to do this evening?" Polly asked, "We could go out for dinner, or just get a takeaway?"

"Why don't we go for a walk while it's still light? You can show me around your local area."

"That sounds like a great idea," replied Polly. She'd been stuck inside either the pub or her flat for most of the day and getting out in the, almost, fresh air for a while was very appealing.

The pair headed out. The clouds looked threatening, but the rain kept at bay for the time being. Mark seemed genuinely interested in hearing about where she lived, and, though nervous to begin with, Polly soon began to enjoy pointing out her local landmarks, like her favourite coffee shop and the lovely old library building she always meant to visit but never seemed to manage to make it into.

As they approached the Bluebell, Polly almost drew attention to it to Mark and suggested they go inside for a drink. She wanted him to see where she worked. Luckily she remembered in time that Mark couldn't know she worked in a pub — it wouldn't be reasonable to suppose she could work full-time and do shifts in the pub and also help Nightingale Farm. She ended up hurrying him past.

"Shall we go in here and grab some food for dinner? I'll cook for you," Mark asked, spotting a Tesco Local.

"You don't have to do that," she insisted, though it was an appealing offer.

"I'd like to. I enjoy cooking, and it's not often I get a night off from farm stuff and can take my time doing it."

"Okay then," agreed Polly.

"You can drink wine and entertain me while I make you my world-famous green Thai fish curry."

"Well, how could I argue with that?"

They went into the supermarket and emerged from it again loaded up with groceries.

It felt fun to be walking home with a man she was having a good time with and to be looking forward to being cooked for and spending the rest of the evening with him.

Soon they were back in the flat and Mark was busy chopping up chillies and onions while Polly poured them both a drink and opened up a packet of pistachio nuts for them to share. Mark really did appear to be enjoying himself as much as she was as he chatted away about the fair and the people he'd met there, as well as some of the beautiful pieces he'd seen which had inspired him. He continued to move further away from the man he had been when he first met her, who'd shouted at her for leaving the farm gate open just a couple of months ago.

They'd just finished eating and were beginning to clear away when Polly's mobile rang; it was Alice.

"Sorry, I better take this," Polly said. "It's my friend, Alice, you met her at the Open Day."

She moved into the sitting room and answered her phone.

"Hey Pol. What are you doing? You don't fancy coming out for a drink, do you?" Alice said.

"Actually, I've just finished having dinner with Mark, he's staying the night," Polly said, taking great delight in awaiting her friend's reaction.

"Mark?"

"Yes, Mark from the farm," Polly clarified.

"I know what Mark! What are you doing with him in your flat, you little minx?"

Polly laughed. "It's nothing like you're imagining I'm sure," she said. "He needed to be in London for a couple of days, so I offered to let him stay at mine."

"And are you hoping for anything to happen . . ."

Polly paused before answering. She would be lying if she said she hadn't thought about what could happen, especially as Mark had become so much friendlier towards her.

"Your silence tells me everything I need to know, honey!" said Alice. "Have an amazing time! Call me tomorrow!"

Alice ended the call before Polly could protest.

She rejoined Mark in the kitchen. His sleeves were rolled up and he was washing the dishes. His arm muscles were impressive — carpentry and farm work must both be a decent upper body workout. Polly felt discombobulated as she realised she longed to go over and touch him and instead busied herself with wiping down the countertop.

"Do you fancy another glass of wine and a movie?"

"Sure, what do you want to watch?"

"How about *Ocean's 11*?" suggested Polly. She'd been meaning to re-watch it for a while.

"Good call," confirmed Mark with a nod.

They moved into the sitting room and sat down next to each other on the sofa. Polly found the movie on Netflix.

"I suspect you're a talker through movies," said Mark as the film was starting. "I'm not."

Polly laughed, she found she now quite liked it when Mark showed a little of his grouchy side. "You'll be pleased to know I don't talk through films, unless there's something really important to say."

"Glad to hear it." He grinned.

They settled down in companionable silence, only stopping to get ice cream and blankets halfway through. The sofa was long and so they had plenty of room, but that didn't mean Polly wasn't extremely aware of him next to her.

When Polly had finished her ice cream, she bent over to place her bowl out of the way, under the sofa.

"There's nowhere to put anything down here," Mark stated. "You need a coffee table or something, doesn't it drive you mad?"

"I suppose it does a bit," said Polly with a shrug. "I guess I haven't got round to buying one yet."

"I've got one you can have," Mark offered gruffly.

"A coffee table you've made you mean?"

"Yeah. It would go well in here."

"I can't accept that . . ." began Polly.

"Don't be ridiculous," Mark rebuffed. "I want you to have it."

"Well, thank you," Polly managed, lost for any other words.

Polly settled back down, pulling her blanket over her. She was well-fed, warm, and getting sleepy, and realised she was feeling the same 'coming home' experience she had when she visited Nightingale Farm. Maybe it wasn't the farm itself, as much as the people in it, and one person in particular, who made her feel that way.

The movie ended and they went to get up at the same time. Their arms touched, sending a delightful shiver through Polly. They both pulled away quickly, keeping their eyes averted from one another.

Mark gave an exaggerated yawn. "Would you mind if I turned in now?" he asked, folding the blankets and still not meeting Polly's eyes.

"Of course not, you use the bathroom first, while I clean up."

They danced awkwardly around each other for the next few minutes until Polly was able to escape to her room.

What had been going on there, she wondered. Had he been worried she'd make a move on him? They'd seemed to be getting along so well before that. She couldn't deny that she fancied Mark, and her feelings for him were only getting stronger as she got to know him better. Sometimes she felt he returned her interest, but she suspected he was as anxious as she was about starting something with someone who was effectively a work colleague. Maybe he'd have time to go for breakfast in the morning and things would become clearer she thought as she got into bed.

* * *

Unfortunately, when Polly got up the next morning, Mark had gone. She'd thought the second day of his trade fair didn't begin until 10 a.m., but it wasn't even eight and his pillows and duvet were neatly folded at the end of the sofa and his bag was gone. Was he trying to avoid her? Had she done something to upset him? She couldn't think of anything.

Then she spotted a note on the kitchen counter.

Hi Polly, thanks for a great evening. Had to leave early for a breakfast meeting with a potential buyer and didn't want to wake you. See you soon. M x

So, though nothing had happened between them the previous evening, that 'x' surely meant there was the possibility of something happening in the future. How could a single 'x' after someone's name make her so happy Polly thought as she struggled to wipe the smile off her face for the rest of the morning.

CHAPTER TEN

Polly had a day where she didn't have a shift at the Bluebell, and she was taking full advantage of the fact that she had nowhere she needed to be, she might as well make the most of not having a job. She treated herself to a lie in and made the executive decision to stay in her softest pyjamas for the whole day — the weather was miserable anyway and if she went out she'd only end up spending money she didn't have.

She was even going to give job hunting a miss — getting nowhere with it was dispiriting and she needed a break.

It was almost 11 a.m. when she settled herself down under a blanket on the sofa, a pillow behind her back, and a hot chocolate in her hands, ready to begin a Netflix marathon.

She was halfway through the second episode of *Sex and the City* when her mobile phone began to ring: her sister's name flashed up on the screen. Polly debated ignoring it, but it could be something important.

"Hi Julie," she said as she answered the call.

"Hi! Guess what?"

"What?" replied Polly absentmindedly as she paused her programme.

"I'm outside your office! What floor are you on? Can you join me for an early lunch?"

113

Damn, Polly thought to herself, options of what she should say racing through her mind.

"I'm not at work," she said honestly.

"Day off? You lucky thing!" Julie replied. "What are you up to?"

"Hanging out at home." Polly looked around the mess that was her flat. She wouldn't be able to put Julie off now her sister knew she had nothing on. She'd have to meet up with her for a bit. But not here. And, above all, she had to try to keep off the topic of her job.

"Why don't I meet you somewhere and we can go for lunch, my treat?" Polly suggested, figuring she could just about afford that, though if her sister chose somewhere pricey, the service her poor car was desperate for would need to wait until after she was paid.

"Great. Shall we meet at Selfridges? We can eat in the Corner Restaurant, I'll call and check they have a table. I'm paying though, I need you to help me choose an outfit for a dinner thing afterwards."

"Sounds good," said Polly, her heart sinking; it would be lovely to be bought a nice lunch, but the shopping trip afterwards would no doubt take hours, and she'd need an awful lot of willpower to get through it credit card intact.

Everything would be a lot easier if she just came clean and admitted to Julie that she'd lost her job, but she still couldn't face it without having a new job to soften the blow. And if she did tell her sister, she'd have to tell her parents too, and they'd be so disappointed. Surely another company would take her on soon.

* * *

An hour later, and Polly was sitting opposite her sister in the stylish art deco-inspired restaurant at a table for two by an enormous window overlooking Oxford Street. They were making short work of a couple of Peach Bellinis when their food arrived: scallops for Julie, and the rather more modestly ordered pasta alla Norma for Polly.

"The children had a wonderful time at the farm last weekend," Julie commented.

"Oh, good . . ."

"It's a great place. They've already asked if we can go back for the strawberry picking."

"Hopefully the farm will have a bumper harvest."

"They enjoyed seeing you too."

Polly immediately registered her sister's judgemental tone — it wasn't hard to spot it, Julie used it a lot around Polly. "It's been a long time since you've visited . . ." Julie continued.

"Yes, I know. I've been busy . . ."

"Too busy for your only niece and nephew?"

"I'm sorry, I'll do better. I promise."

Polly's apology seemed to placate Julie.

"And I'll make sure I pop in to see Mum and Dad too," said Polly, before her sister could start on her second favourite topic of conversation.

"So, how's work?" asked Julie.

"Busy," Polly replied quickly. "How's . . . everything with you?"

"Fine," said Julie with a shrug. "You know, same old, same old. Phil's taken over another fund, which is why I need a new dress — there's a big shebang being organised."

"That sounds fun!" Polly said.

Julie gave a weak smile. "I think I'd rather have a movie and pizza night with Phil and the kids, to be honest, but it's fine."

That definitely didn't sound like her sister, who usually relished any opportunity to get dressed up and go somewhere special, but Polly guessed anyone would get bored of glitzy night outs after a while.

"Any idea what kind of dress you want?" she asked, hoping to get Julie more excited about Phil's special night.

"There was the most amazing Alexander McQueen mini dress in *Vogue* this month, but I think something from Ted Baker or Whistles will be more within my budget," Julie said.

"Do you need shoes as well?"

Julie nodded. "Probably . . . and maybe a clutch."

It felt like a lifetime ago to Polly since she'd been clothes shopping. Ironically, back when she'd actually had the money to spend on buying beautiful things for herself, she didn't have the time or energy to do so because she was working so hard and such long hours.

"Oh, can you recommend someone from your firm to help out a friend of Phil's?" asked Julie. "I meant to message you about it last week actually."

Polly froze, fork full of pasta mid-air. "Um . . . well . . ." How was she going to get out of this one? If she gave Julie the details of someone working at Streamline her sister would surely tell Phil's friend to mention Polly when they called and her secret would be well and truly out of the bag. Why had she even started lying in the first place?

"Is that a problem?" Julie said, giving Polly a confused look.

"It's just that things are really crazy at work at the moment. I don't think we're taking on any new clients."

"Oh, okay," said Julie with a shrug. "That's good for you if Streamline's so popular. Do you think you'll finally get a promotion soon?"

There you go. That kind of comment was exactly the reason why Polly had decided not to come clean when she was first made redundant. She was certain Julie didn't mean it, and she was guilty of reading too much into some of her sister's comments, but Julie so often made Polly feel like she wasn't good enough and was being left behind in life.

Once they'd finished their delicious meals, they wandered out of the restaurant, and into the women's clothing area. A personal shopper came over to greet them, but was politely shooed away by Julie. "I don't have time for all that," she explained to Polly, "I've got to pick up Olivia in a couple of hours."

Julie was impressive to watch as she marched around the department, ruthlessly discarding dresses left, right and centre. Polly trailed after her.

"This one I think," Julie declared after only a few minutes when she pounced on a black, mid-length, one-shouldered cocktail dress. "Hold my bag," Julie said, and disappeared into the changing room. She emerged again a few minutes later.

"How was it?" Polly asked.

"It fits," said Julie. "I've got a clutch that'll match, but I may as well get shoes as Phil's buying."

Julie paid, and they walked through to the shoe department. "What the hell," Julie muttered, grabbing a pair of black patent Louboutins with a killer heel. "Can I get these in a six, please?" she asked an assistant. In a flash, the shoes were produced and Julie had handed over her card. "There's no need to try them on," Julie explained. "They're Louboutins."

"Done!" Julie declared as they turned from the cash register. "Right, what do you need?"

"I'm good, I don't need anything," Polly said.

"You must need something!"

"Actually, to be honest, money's a bit tight at the moment . . ." admitted Polly.

"Would a loan help?" asked her big sister immediately, making Polly smile — whatever other faults Julie may have, she was unfailingly generous.

"No, thank you. Honestly, I'm fine, I just can't afford to buy Louboutins. I can run to treating my niece and nephew to a cupcake each from the food hall though."

"They'd love that."

The two sisters headed to Lola's Cupcakes for two Chocolate Heaven treats before walking to the tube station together and going off in different directions.

Polly sunk into her seat on the Underground, pleasantly surprised at how much she'd enjoyed the last few hours. It really had been too long since she and Julie had done something like that together. Possibly not since before the children had been born. She needed to check in with her sister more, she hadn't seemed quite herself today. Polly wondered if Julie and Phil were having marriage problems . . . She'd have hoped that Julie would confide in her if she needed to, but maybe not. After all, Polly herself hadn't exactly been forthcoming about her own problems lately, had she?

* * *

Polly was checking her emails a few days later when she spotted one which made her heart skip a beat. She opened it quickly: the completed holiday cottage had its first booking! A couple had booked to stay for the following weekend, taking advantage of a special offer they'd made available to anyone wanting to stay in the next month.

She immediately picked up her phone to call Mark — he'd worked so hard to get it ready quickly, she had to let him know right away. Plus, it was the excuse she'd secretly been waiting for to contact him.

He picked up on the second ring. "Polly, hi! How are you?" he asked, cheerfully.

"I'm good. I'm calling because you've got your first booking for the cottage!"

"Oh, wow!"

"They're arriving next Friday afternoon and staying for two nights."

Mark went quiet.

"Is everything okay?" Polly checked.

"Yeah, it's brilliant news. I'm just thinking about what needs to get done before they arrive."

"Would you like me to come down and help?" asked Polly.

"I couldn't ask you to do that . . ." Mark replied, unconvincingly.

"They won't be with you until after three because that's when we've set the check-in time. I can get to you in the morning and give you a hand with the finishing touches."

"What about your work?"

"Don't worry about that," said Polly, feeling awkward. "I'll sort it out."

"Well, if you're sure, that would be amazing," admitted Mark.

"Absolutely. I'll see you Friday. Oh, and could you let Maggie know the guests have ordered a breakfast basket from her."

"Of course. Thanks again."

A smile broke out across Polly's face as she put her mobile down. Now she just had to rearrange her shifts at the Bluebell, again . . .

It was so exciting to think things were really starting to change at Nightingale Farm — and at least some of that was down to her. She was proud of that and was looking forward to helping to put the final touches to the cottage before its first guests arrive. She already had lists running through her head of everything that would need to be checked and the little extras that would make their visitors feel special and would hopefully lead to their first 5-star TripAdvisor review.

CHAPTER ELEVEN

Polly was up bright and early on Friday morning, eager to be off to Nightingale Farm. Another booking had come through for the cottage for three nights this time, and the cottage next to it was nearly ready to be advertised as a holiday let. She'd stay Friday night and give Mark a hand with painting the second cottage and putting curtains and furniture in place. Hopefully, she'd be able to take photos and get them online when she was home on Sunday before she started her shift at the pub.

Mark and Dylan were waiting for her in the yard when she arrived, Mark pacing back and forth.

"Where's your dad?" Polly asked, making a fuss of the dog and looking around for John.

"He's at Maggie's house. She needed some help with her garden." The twinkle in Mark's eyes made it clear he was very pleased Maggie and his father were getting on so well, and Polly couldn't help but agree; John so deserved to be happy, and they made a lovely couple. "They'll be back this afternoon to prepare for the weekend's visitors. We're expecting quite a few people, if the interest on Facebook is anything to go by.

"That's excellent!" She beamed.

"It is. Would you like a cup of tea, or shall we go straight up to the cottage?"

"Let's get to work," said Polly. "I want to see how much there is to do. And there's always the danger that the couple may arrive early . . ."

The panic on Mark's face made Polly quickly add, "But that's really unlikely to happen."

"Let's go," said Mark, firmly. "Dylan, you can come too, but don't you dare put dirty paw prints on everything!"

Polly was marched over to the completed cottage, Dylan hurrying her along as much as Mark. Of course, it looked lovely, scrupulously neat and clean. It just needed a little bit of a woman's touch, she thought.

While Mark made up the beds with the new linen, Polly pottered around downstairs, rearranging the furniture, plumping cushions, and generally making everything look welcoming. She did an inventory check and made a list of anything that was missing — washing up liquid for one thing.

Polly moved upstairs and worked her way around while Mark went to fill the large basket by the wood burner in the sitting room with a fresh supply of seasoned logs.

"I need to head out to the shops to grab a few extra bits," Polly said.

"I'll drive if you like," offered Mark. Seeing Polly's surprise at his suggestion led him to add, "Hopefully we'll have lots more visitors and I'm going to have to learn how to set the cottages up by myself, you can't always be coming to bail me out, so I'd better see what I need to buy in the future."

"Fair enough," agreed Polly. "Let's get going then."

At Mark's battered old Land Rover, he grabbed a load of paper and random stuff which had built up in the passenger seat and chucked it in the back.

"Your chariot, my lady," he said, grandly. "Dylan, you'll have to stay here."

Dylan's ears went down and his tail drooped.

"Tash and Clive are in the barn, go and help them!" Mark suggested. Dylan perked up again and went trotting off in search of his friends.

"That dog is far too intelligent for his own good," muttered Mark.

Polly climbed in the car and they set off.

They drove for about fifteen minutes until they reached a large roundabout and Polly saw a sign for a Tesco Extra located off one of the exits.

"Please tell me we're not heading towards a huge supermarket?" she asked.

"Why not? It'll have everything we need."

"First of all, you're a small, local business, you should be supporting other small, local businesses, who will, in turn, recommend you to people, and maybe even stock your products eventually. Secondly, how special is it for people to find the same boring old soap in their holiday cottage as they have by their kitchen sink at home?"

"Okay, you make some good points," admitted Mark. He took a different turning heading towards a little town named Stoutbridge which Polly had never visited before.

Leaving the Land Rover in the town's car park, they headed straight to a local health food shop Polly had heard of, and which she'd seen had also started following the farm's Facebook page.

"They've got lots of zero waste and plastic-free products I think visitors will like," she explained.

They picked up some English breakfast teabags, freshly ground coffee, and a selection box of herbal teas.

Glass dispensers were bought and refill containers of liquid soap made by a local business to fill them with. Polly got the owner's business card — thinking she might be interested in having a stall at the Christmas Fair the farm was planning.

They picked up refillable bottles of surface cleaner, washing up liquid, and some cleaning cloths made from bamboo. Polly knew that tea towels and bath towels had already been chosen by John and Maggie.

Next, Polly dragged Mark into three charity shops in a row. She scoured them all for popular books in good condition, a mixture from *Harry Potter* to *Pride and Prejudice* and *The Girl on the Train* — hopefully there'd be something to suit anyone who stayed — and they could always add to the collection over time. And, of course, there would need to be more for the other cottages.

The completed cottage had a small television with a built-in DVD player in the sitting room, so Polly also began work on a DVD collection for the cottages. Again, she went for a broad selection, hoping anyone could find something they fancied as the holiday homes would only have basic TV channels and it was a cheaper option than providing Netflix, at least for the moment.

By the time they popped into the bakery and bought a pasty each to refuel, Mark was so laden down with bags, he looked more like a pack horse than a carpenter cum farmer.

They got back in the Land Rover gratefully dumping all their purchases on the back seat. Then they walked to a little park close by and got coffees from the café there before settling down on a bench to enjoy their lunch. The skies were grey, but it was dry and warm enough to be outside.

"It's almost one," said Mark, checking his watch.

"Don't worry," Polly soothed. "We've got one more quick stop to make and then it won't take long to finish off the cottage when we're back."

Once they'd finished eating they returned to the car and Polly directed Mark to a garden centre she'd spotted on the outskirts of the town. She knew exactly what she was after, so ran in by herself to save time and re-emerged a few minutes later with a selection of houseplants to dot around the cottage.

"Trust me," she said. "These will finish the house off, and they're all super easy to take care of. Not that that should be a problem with your dad around, but still . . ."

It was just gone two o'clock when they returned to the farm. They waved hello to John, who was restocking the shop with fruit and veg ready for the weekend, and carried on down the much-improved lane to the cottages.

It was quarter to three when Polly stepped back to admire her handiwork, satisfied she'd done the best she could; the cottage definitely had a calm, homely feel to it. She took some photos on her phone of the final result to post on the farm's Facebook page and to update the cottage's Airbnb listing.

Mark had left her with the keys to the other properties, so Polly took the opportunity to have a look over those too. The second cottage was a cosy one-bedroom, perfect for a couple's romantic getaway. The kitchen and sitting room had been knocked into one large room downstairs. There was a double bedroom and bathroom upstairs. A patio area out the back surrounded by ivy-covered stone walls contained a cast-iron table and chairs set and barbecue under a covering, and potted plants were dotted around.

Polly was impressed by how much had been done — it was just a matter of a few days' work before this cottage would be ready for visitors. Once John and Mark got their teeth into something, it seemed they followed through.

Work had started on the third and fourth cottages but was not very far along. Polly thought she'd suggest they focus on the cottage at the end of the row — it was the largest with three bedrooms, so would add more variety to what they could offer. She made a note to pick up a selection of board games and children's toys for it.

She locked up and wandered back to the farmhouse. She was just in time to see a silver car arrive and pull up outside the animal shed. Mark quickly appeared and Polly saw him hand some keys through the open car window and point the way to the cottages.

"I take it that was the VIPs?" said Polly, smiling.

"Yeah," Mark replied. "They seem nice. I said I'd go down and meet them there to show them how everything works. You'll stay for supper, won't you?"

"Sure. I've got a few things I wanted to go over with you and your dad anyway, so I thought I'd stay the night, if that's alright?"

"Great, I'll come and find you in a while." Mark smiled at Polly, making her own face light up.

Polly walked over to see Maggie in her tearoom. Maggie was also setting up for the weekend but took a break to make lattes and freshly toasted teacakes smothered with butter for them both.

It was amazing how easily Maggie had fitted into the farm set-up, especially when it came to her friendship with John, Polly thought. Her little café and her personality suited the place so well.

Polly helped Maggie hang some vintage kitchen signs on the wall behind the counter, and make some space for more tables to cater for how popular the café was proving.

"Are you heading home now, Maggie?" Polly asked when they were all done.

"Yep. I've got an evening with my cat and a few old episodes of *Downton Abbey* planned. I can't wait to get my feet up. John asked if I'd like to stay for food, but Sue's coming and something tells me she's not my biggest fan."

Polly felt her heart sink. "In fairness, she doesn't seem to like anyone. I wouldn't take it personally." She gave Maggie a conspiratorial smile.

"Oh, I won't!" Maggie replied, laughing. "I just don't fancy being glared at for the next few hours."

"Can't say I blame you. If Mark had mentioned Sue was coming, I might not have been as quick as I was in accepting his invitation," Polly admitted.

"You and Mark are certainly getting along well. I hear you went shopping for home goods together today," commented Maggie, her eyes twinkling.

"I guess he's not quite as prickly as I originally thought," laughed Polly.

"He's got a lot on his mind, that's all," said Maggie, wisely. "But the changes you've helped to make here have made the world of difference."

Polly hugged Maggie in thanks for her kind words. She was so proud of the farm's transformation, and her part in it.

Polly was just closing the farm gate behind Maggie's departing car when she saw Aunt Sue's car in the distance. She reopened it and waited patiently while Sue took at least twice as long as she surely needed to drive through.

Aunt Sue then spent ages fussing around parking up and fiddling around inside her car while Polly stood awkwardly, not wanting to appear rude by walking off and not saying a proper hello.

Finally, Sue emerged from her vehicle. "What are you looking so pleased about?" she asked, mock-sweetly.

Still revelling in Maggie's lovely comments, Polly replied, "It's a big day for the farm. The first guests have just arrived and Mark and I had a really good afternoon getting the last things for the completed cottage."

Polly was sure she glimpsed a grimace on Sue's face which she swiftly hid with a sickly smile. "So, it's Mark who's got you grinning like a Cheshire cat! Has that naughty nephew of mine been flirting with you?" asked Aunt Sue, beginning to laugh nastily. "That boy! He's probably hoping for a discount on your rates!"

Polly's expression must have given at least a hint of the confusion she felt, because Sue continued, "Oh dear! Surely you didn't think he actually liked you?" She paused, delighting in Polly's confusion. "I'm so cross with him for leading you on! Especially when he's dating my goddaughter, Sophia. Sophia's mother and I have been desperate to set them up for years and we're so glad it's finally happened. They make such a lovely couple."

Sue peered at Polly intensely. "Oh no! Don't tell me that wicked boy failed to tell you he was in a relationship?"

Polly didn't know what to say. She felt like a complete idiot. She'd genuinely believed Mark liked her. Why hadn't he mentioned that he had a girlfriend? She knew she'd never asked him outright about his single status, but surely he should have brought it up. Or had his attraction to her been all in her head? No, it had seemed like he was flirting with her, she was sure she hadn't been imagining it. She couldn't believe that he'd been after a discount like Sue suggested, so was he just leading her on for his own amusement? That must be the only explanation. And to have to be told by Aunt Sue of all people! But surely John would have said something . . . Unless Mark had asked him not to of course . . . That thought hurt almost as much as Mark lying to her.

"Who Mark dates is none of my business," Polly said with as little emotion as she could manage. "Our relationship is purely professional."

Aunt Sue gave a smirk: it was obvious she didn't believe Polly for a minute.

"Well, that's good because Sophia will be here any minute now," Aunt Sue continued gleefully. "You'll be able to see for yourself how perfect she and Mark look together."

"Wonderful," Polly replied, forcing a smile on her face in a valiant attempt to hold back the tears she could feel threatening to fall.

With another satisfied sneer, Aunt Sue said, "Well, I'd better be getting inside," and marched into the house.

It only took Polly a second to confirm to herself that she was leaving. She wasn't going to put herself through an evening sitting opposite Mark and Sophia, watching them all over each other and feeling even more of an idiot than she already did.

She wished Maggie were still here to help her quickly come up with an excuse to leave.

"Hello, love," John called, appearing from around the side of the house.

"Hi," Polly replied as cheerfully as she could manage. "I'm really sorry, but I'm going to have to shoot off. I've got so much work I need to catch up on."

"We haven't taken up too much of your time, have we?" asked John looking concerned.

"No, not at all, I was happy to come today," reassured Polly. "Will you give my apologies to Mark?"

"Of course,' he replied, now looking disappointed. "Hopefully you can pop down to see us again soon."

"Hopefully," agreed Polly. Swiftly blinking back the tears in her eyes, she hurried to her car.

CHAPTER TWELVE

As much as it pained Polly to stay away from the farm, and Mark in particular, she knew she needed to for her own self-preservation. Of course, she'd never abandon John, but she kept contact to the bare minimum, using email wherever possible and ignoring the WhatsApp messages Mark had sent her with updates on Bubble and Squeak until they'd stopped coming. It had been nearly three months and she kept up the claim that she was completely snowed under with work and simply couldn't get away to visit the farm in person. She didn't think John was totally convinced by this but suspected he was too polite to question her.

She wondered if Mark thought about her, or whether whatever she'd felt had been between them was completely in her head. It had probably been a bit of fun for him at the most, a distraction from all the work he'd been putting in at the farm. She wished she could let go of him, but no matter how often she told herself to forget about him, he always seemed to be on her mind.

The good news was that Nightingale Farm was doing brilliantly: visitors absolutely loved it. John's market garden was flourishing and both the farm shop and the farmer's markets he was selling at were bringing in a steady income.

All four of the cottages were finished and were fully booked for the summer holidays. The TripAdvisor reviews were really positive.

Tash and Clive were now permanent members of staff, there every day the farm was open to the public, leaving John more time for his gardening and Mark for his carpentry. Apparently, Mark now had part of his workshop set aside as more of a showroom, and he'd made some big sales from farm visitors wandering in. She'd seen photos of him on the farm's Facebook page, which Tash was now updating, and thought he looked happy.

Polly hadn't been presented with any final figures yet, Sue was still very definitely in charge of those, but the farm looked set to make a profit for the year, even with the expense of renovating the cottages.

* * *

Polly had an earlier start than she was used to, Alice had been really busy at the estate agency and with renovating her house, and so the friends hadn't seen each other for weeks. They'd decided to meet for breakfast before Alice headed off to work.

Eschewing the fancier coffee shops along Clapham Junction, the pair chose a table in the sunshine outside their favourite greasy spoon, and ordered full English breakfasts and mugs of builder's tea.

They chatted about the new kitchen being put in to Alice's house until their food arrived and Alice asked, "So, how are things with you?"

"Same old, really," Polly replied.

Alice's forehead creased in concern, "No job leads then?"

"I've got an interview later actually."

"That's great, what's the job?"

"It's with some marketing consultancy firm."

"You don't seem very excited about it."

"I'm not," admitted Polly. "But at least it's closer to what I want to do than working in the Bluebell."

130

They ate in silence until Alice asked, "So what about the farm? How's it doing? I'm guessing you haven't heard from Mark."

Hearing Mark's name said aloud sent a jolt through Polly's body and her breath caught in her throat.

"The farm's good," she finally managed to reply. "Great, actually. It's doing so well. . . Mark emails me about anything important, but we haven't chatted. To be honest, I still feel like a total idiot for liking him so much. I read the situation completely wrong and built a little fantasy in my head."

"I saw you two together, remember?" said Alice. "I was sure he liked you. From what you said about him, he didn't seem the sort to mess you around."

"I didn't think so either, but there you go," Polly said with a shrug. "Do you mind if we change the subject?"

"Of course not," said her friend, kindly. "Did I tell you about the house I went to value last week with the dungeon in the basement?"

Polly smiled, her best friend always knew how to cheer her up. She just wished Alice had a permanent solution for helping her over her heartache, because giving it time just didn't seem to be working.

* * *

Polly honestly didn't hold out a lot of hope for her interview that afternoon. She'd been to so many since her redundancy and hadn't got anywhere. It was hard not to get despondent and to retain any hope that this interview would end differently from all the others.

Polly was taking her best suit out of the wardrobe in preparation when her phone rang. The farm's number flashed up on the screen. She knew it would be John, Mark hadn't called her since the afternoon she was last at Nightingale Farm, the day of their shopping trip, but her stomach still gave an involuntary flip at the small possibility that it could be Mark at the end of the line.

She answered.

"Hello, love," said John's voice. She felt a wave of disappointment that she'd been right, and then felt terribly guilty: she shouldn't be disappointed to be speaking to John!

"Hello John," Polly cheerfully replied. "How are you?"

"I'm good. Things have been busy here."

"That's brilliant. The bookings for the cottages are fantastic. As soon as Sue gets the figures over to me, I can work out your profit since we began implementing all the changes, and figure out if there's stuff that's not working or anything you should be doing more."

"Actually, that's sort of why I'm calling," John said hesitantly. "Sue dropped some more figures round to us last night after Mark had a word with her. Mark was going to scan them with his phone or something so he could send them to you, but I had a little look at them first, and they don't seem to add up, and Mark agrees. He's been working out our income and outgoings roughly, and we should have made a lot more than we have. I can't fathom what's happened. We've worked so hard, and it all seemed to be going well. We've had lots of visitors and the cottages have been popular . . ."

Polly was puzzled. What could have gone wrong? Had they vastly overspent on renovating the cottages without realising? Or was it caring for the new animals that was costing more than expected? She'd have to go to the farm. There was no way she could go through everything with John over the phone, and if there was a problem with the farm's finances, she needed to get to the bottom of it straight away before it could get any worse. "I can't come today, but I can be with you after lunch tomorrow. Is that alright?"

"Thank you," said John, sounding relieved. "That would be great,"

"No problem. I've got to go now, but I'll see you tomorrow and I'm sure we can straighten it all out. It's probably just a little error somewhere."

She got dressed in a daze, her mind on the farm, wishing she didn't have the interview to go to. She'd much rather drive straight to the farm and begin going through the accounts with a fine-toothed comb, even if that meant seeing Mark.

They must have made a profit! Yes, they'd had a lot of outgoings to deal with, an awful lot of outgoings, but the sale of the land should have covered all of that — at least that had been the plan. Had she vastly underestimated how much things would cost? Not properly accounted for the wages of the staff they'd employed? Yet Polly was sure she'd been so careful with her calculations, definitely erring on the side of extreme caution when it came to ensuring all costs would be covered.

But, she scolded herself, she hadn't actually seen what was going on at the farm for months. She'd let her hurt pride at feeling misled by Mark blind her to what she should have been doing: ensuring everything was running smoothly at Nightingale Farm. She hadn't even been chasing Aunt Sue for the accounts, which she should have been seeing regularly, because she felt so humiliated talking to her.

Going through the motions of preparing for her interview, Polly's head remained at Nightingale Farm. She even considered cancelling the interview, or at least calling to check if the company would agree to reschedule it. She knew how unprofessional that would make her look though . . . and she'd be able to see the figures the next day. A few hours wouldn't make a difference to the fate of the farm, surely?

* * *

Polly felt the interview went well, but she'd put it completely out of her mind by the following morning when she took the opportunity to go over her business plans for the farm and the notes she'd made since she'd started implementing her changes. She still couldn't find anything amiss, certainly nothing that would make a big difference to the farm's finances. This did nothing to calm her nerves though — what if she'd made a mistake or a miscalculation which messed everything up for John and Mark? She'd never forgive herself if they lost their family home because of her.

Her stomach in knots, she drove to the farm. Her Volvo was making even louder squeaks and clunks than usual which didn't exactly help her to relax. She made a mental note that she'd have to finally book it in for a service when she got home.

Polly was only about two miles away from the farm when her car gave one final ominous clunk and the engine cut out. Thankfully Polly was going slowly enough that she was able to steer it into a turning spot on the country lane before grounding to a halt.

What terrible luck! What should she do? Her first thought was to phone a breakdown company, but she didn't have cover anymore, she'd let it slip when she had to cut back on everything after losing her job. So now she'd have to ring a local garage and get a tow. She groaned inwardly, it would cost a small fortune.

She couldn't call her mum and dad or her sister to rescue her because how would she explain her being on her way to Nightingale Farm in the middle of a workday? Also, none of them had a tow bar so she'd still have to deal with getting the car to a garage.

Of course, there was always option number three: get in touch with John and ask him for help. But she was supposed to be professional, this was supposed to be a business relationship. She couldn't ring him for a favour like he was one of her friends, especially after what had happened with Mark. The problem was that she did think of John as a friend. She wouldn't hesitate to help him if he were in a pickle, and she was sure he felt the same way about her. But he was Mark's father. She was embarrassed that Aunt Sue had felt the need to put her straight about Mark and Sophia, so embarrassed, but more than that she was hurt. Hurt that Mark, who she'd trusted and who'd genuinely appeared to be a good guy, had treated her like he had.

Resolved to have to take on yet more shifts at the pub, she got out her mobile to Google the number of a local garage and was dismayed to discover the signal didn't look like it would be strong enough to make a call. Stupid countryside! She'd have to walk along the road until she reached a patch of good signal. To top it all off, it had started to rain.

Polly was about to set off when she heard another vehicle approaching. Her heart leapt when she saw it was Mark's Land Rover, being driven by the man himself. He pulled over behind her car and got out. Annoyingly, he was still as good-looking as ever.

"Hey," he said, pushing his hair out of his eyes as he approached her. He cleared his throat, looking a little wary. "Dad said you were on your way to the farm. Is everything okay?"

Polly considered telling him that everything was fine and she'd just stopped to admire the view so he'd leave and she wouldn't have to deal with talking to him, but she wasn't sure he'd believe her and she was pretty stuck.

"My car's broken down," she explained. "It's been making some weird noises, and I meant to get it checked out . . ." The truth was that Polly had been using the car as little as possible and turning the radio up louder and louder to drown out the car's clunks and whines when she absolutely had to drive it.

"Would you like me to have a look?" Mark asked.

"Yes, please," mumbled Polly, really not happy to be accepting his help, but not seeing there was another sensible option.

"Pop the bonnet for me, and I'll see what I can do."

Polly did as instructed and Mark poked and prodded around for a few minutes.

"I can't fix it here," Mark said finally. "Let's get it towed back to the farm and I should be able to get it going again."

She was grateful for his assistance, but wished it was anyone other than him helping her. "Thank you," she managed to say.

Mark took out a tow rope and attached it to the front of Polly's car. Tying the other end to the towage on his Land Rover, he instructed Polly to get in her car so she could steer and they set off at a snail's pace to the farm.

The short journey seemed to take forever, but at least she wasn't in his car having to make polite conversation Polly mused.

Dylan was beside himself with happiness at seeing Polly when they reached the farm, and there was no hope of her being able to do anything until he'd been made a proper fuss of. Once he'd been petted and he'd finally calmed down, Polly took out her mobile. The signal was much improved in the yard, and she offered to call a garage from there.

"If you'd rather," Mark said with a shrug and walked off towards his workshop, which naturally made Polly feel like she'd been terribly rude. She hadn't meant to be. She knew Mark had a lot on his plate, she'd have thought that looking over her car was the last thing he'd want to do, or that he'd have time for. She was sure she'd insulted him but didn't know what to say to make it better. Should she go after him and apologise?

Her dilemma was pushed to the back of her mind when John appeared at the front door of the farmhouse. He looked thrilled to see her, "Come in out of the rain, love," he called out. Then he spotted her car attached to Mark's. "What happened to your car?" he asked, aghast.

"I'm not sure," Polly replied. "It just cut out. Luckily Mark came along and gave me a tow because I didn't have any mobile signal to call for help."

"Is he going to have a look at it for you?"

"He offered to," Polly said quickly, "but I don't want to put him out. I'll call a garage, they can tow it back to London and give me a lift home."

"It's no trouble for him to look, Mark's good with engines. There are some mornings I can't believe he manages to get our tractor going . . ."

"It'll be easier for me to call the garage and get it back to London," said Polly firmly. If the car couldn't be fixed by Mark today, she'd end up having to be driven home by him and would need to pick the car up somehow when it was ready . . . it was all getting increasingly complicated.

"Alright, love, if you're sure," said John kindly. "Thank you so much for coming down so quickly. Let's get you set up with all these numbers, shall we?"

Polly followed him into the house and called her local garage while John made her a cup of tea. She gave them directions to the farm, and they said they'd be with her in a couple of hours.

John had the accounts for the last year ready on the kitchen table for her. She settled down with them while he went back out to his garden. She immediately began spotting discrepancies everywhere. It was all done very sneakily — amounts recorded for a far higher amount than corresponding receipts and a lot of cash withdrawals filed under 'miscellaneous' — John and Mark both had bank cards for anything to do with the farm, they would rarely need to use cash and Polly had asked them not to whenever possible so it was easier to keep track of expenses. The cash was being withdrawn almost daily from a cash machine, and she knew neither Mark nor John visited the town that often.

It seemed there could only be one explanation; someone had been skimming off the profits. There was no way either John or Mark would steal from the farm's money, of that Polly was certain. There was only one other person who had access to the accounts: Aunt Sue.

After about an hour, John came in to check how she was getting on and Polly took the opportunity to ask to see any older accounts he could easily get his hands on. John disappeared into the little office space next to the sitting room and reappeared a while later laden down with all the paperwork going back to before his wife inherited the farm.

"I think I'm getting somewhere," Polly said. "Would you mind if I took this lot back home? I'll only need it for a couple of days?"

"Sure," replied John. He twisted his wedding ring anxiously.

"Please don't worry," said Polly quickly, desperate to reassure him. It wouldn't be right to accuse Sue of underhand dealing unless she was absolutely sure that's what had been going on. Polly knew she'd be able to relax more at home and take her time and would hopefully find the proof she needed to work out what had gone wrong with the farm's finances.

* * *

The beep of the breakdown vehicle's horn pulled Polly away from the piles of paper still spread out in front of her. She was pleased they'd arrived, she felt awkward discovering what she had while sitting at the farmhouse's kitchen table. She'd be happier by herself, and away from John's worried eyes.

Her car was swiftly winched up onto the back of the truck, and she collected up all the papers into a Bag for Life which John gave her and which somehow only served to make the whole situation all the sadder.

* * *

Back in her flat, Polly didn't even bother to take off her coat and shoes before she delved back into the accounts. She made meticulous notes, her evidence had to be completely irrefutable.

Of course, John and Mark would be upset when they discovered what Sue had done, but they had to know. If Sue carried on the way she was, the farm was in danger of getting itself back in the very precarious financial situation she'd originally found it in. Only this time, there was no extra land for them to be able to sell off.

Polly was furious: she'd never liked her, but would never have believed Sue could be capable of systematically stealing from her own brother and nephew over several years. Polly knew that John paid her well for her work with the accounts, she didn't do it out of the goodness of her own heart. Sue had taken advantage of the fact that John had been so stressed about the farm, that he'd been too full of grief and worry to examine the figures closely and to ask her about anything that didn't look right. He would never have known that his own sister was contributing to his financial problems. Sue had kept most of the information to herself, and what she did share, Polly suspected had been shoved in a drawer out of the way by John.

Now she'd collected all her evidence together, she was faced with the terrible prospect of having to break the news to John.

CHAPTER THIRTEEN

Polly felt she must tell John what she'd discovered in person, but that had to wait a couple of days until her car was back on the road. As soon as she'd received the call from the garage to let her know her car was ready to be picked up, she phoned John and asked if he was free for her to come to the farm and go over the accounts with him that afternoon.

"How bad is it?" he'd asked and Polly could hear the anxiety in his voice.

"It's nothing we can't sort out," said Polly, honestly. "You're not going to lose the farm. I'll fill you in properly when I see you."

* * *

John was waiting in the farmyard when Polly arrived. She felt dreadful to be the bearer of bad news, but at least John would know the truth and they could get the farm's finances properly under control.

Polly could tell John was desperate for her to give him the verdict, yet he'd never be so rude as to not make her a cup of tea and get out the biscuit tin first. The kettle had just finished boiling when Mark came in from outside. He gave Polly a curt nod of acknowledgement before washing his hands and sitting as far away from her it seemed as possible. She decided to ignore him. Or at least attempt to ignore him. She had more important things to concentrate on, she told herself.

She spread the evidence she'd collected out in front of her and was about to begin taking John and Mark through her findings when the sound of an indignant car horn interrupted her. Without a word, Mark got up to see who had arrived.

They heard the farm gate being opened and then closed again after a car drove through.

A moment later Mark reappeared at the kitchen door closely followed by his aunt.

Aunt Sue's face was dark as thunder and she looked ready for a fight.

"Sue!" John said, sounding surprised. "How nice to see you. Would you like a cuppa?"

"No, thank you," replied Sue curtly. "I won't be staying long. Luckily I phoned earlier and Mark told me what was going to be happening here. As the business' bookkeeper, I thought I ought to be present to see how Little Miss Fix-It here attempts to worm her way out of the mess she's made of this place."

"My suggestions worked," Polly wasn't able to stop herself from saying. "They're the reason this place is still in business."

"A likely story," Sue retorted. "Don't forget, I've seen the accounts. I know how much those cottages cost to renovate, and what goes out to feed all the new animals you *insisted* the farm needed to take on."

"All the work was within budget," Polly said firmly.

"Oh, really? Have you seen the amount she threw about on organic rubbish for the cottages? Got a bit of a deal going on with the woman who runs that ridiculously overpriced hippy shop? You know she called here? You really should have given her your private number."

"Sue!" said John, sounding mortified. "I'm sure there's nothing untoward going on!"

"Oh, really . . ." said Aunt Sue before Polly could get over the shock of her accusation to refute it. "Then why has she been lying for months, telling you she's got some high-powered city job? She got fired from that job long before she started messing things up around here."

Aunt Sue looked at her triumphantly.

"Don't be ridiculous," said Mark, and Polly's heart leapt at him defending her, but sank again as she realised all her lies were about to be revealed.

Sue looked at Polly, her eyes gleaming, luxuriating in tormenting her prey. "I thought there might be something going on when Polly was spending so much time here. Surely someone with such an important career wouldn't be able to hang around the farm lusting after my nephew in the middle of the working day. So I did a little investigating, looked her up on LinkedIn, and gave her employers a call, or should I say her *former* employers. They told me she'd been fired back in January."

"I wasn't fired!" interrupted Polly, hotly. "I was made redundant."

"Do excuse me if I don't believe anything you have to say," retorted Aunt Sue sharply.

"Is this true?" John asked quietly. He sounded breathless, Polly realised with concern.

"Yes," she admitted, and quickly tried to explain, "I didn't think you'd take me seriously if you knew I'd lost my job, and I hadn't told my family yet so I didn't want the news getting back to them."

"Why wouldn't you tell your family?" John questioned.

Polly did her very best to block Aunt Sue out as she focused on answering John. "I was embarrassed. I'd made a really big deal about my job and I was disposed of in the blink of an eye. I planned to get another, ideally even better, job, quickly, but that didn't happen."

"Of course, it didn't happen!" snorted Aunt Sue. "If the mess you've made of this place is anything to go by, you probably lied yourself into the job in the first place and they got rid of you the first opportunity they could!"

"Let's just try to calm down and talk things through," John said. His face deathly pale, he stood up in an attempt to get Sue and Polly's attention. It didn't work.

"I did not mess up the farm's finances!" retorted Polly. "That was all you! You've been stealing from the farm for years!"

Sue's smirk faltered for a second, but she swiftly composed herself. "You think I'd steal from my own brother? That's what you're accusing me of?"

"Yes!"

Suddenly there was a crash. Polly's head turned instinctively towards it. John was lying on the floor, clutching his chest. In an instant, everyone was around him.

"I'll call an ambulance," Mark said, the colour drained from his face. He took his mobile out of his pocket and began dialling, his hand shaking.

Polly's animosity towards Sue was forgotten as she crouched on the floor speaking calmly to John, explaining that help was coming.

"Get out of the way," Sue snapped, bringing a cushion to lay under John's head.

Polly stood back up. "Can I do anything?" she asked Mark, ignoring Sue.

"You've caused quite enough harm to this family," hissed Aunt Sue in response. "The best thing you could do is leave."

Polly looked to Mark for support. He knew how much his father meant to her. "I think that might be for the best," he said distractedly, before turning to focus on John. "I'll message you later to let you know how he is."

Heartbroken, Polly left the farm, leaving all her carefully prepared paperwork behind.

* * *

Polly drove back to her flat in a daze, putting the kettle on as soon as she got in, more for something to do than for any actual need for a drink. She waited impatiently for it to boil then remembered she hadn't even taken off her jacket or shoes.

She turned her mobile on loud so there was no way she'd miss a text about John and did her best to distract herself by making her tea and giving the kitchen a wipe down, but her eyes kept constantly flashing to her phone.

Though hopeful about the previous day's interview, she'd got her hopes up about others before only to be disappointed, and so, trying to continue with some form of normality, Polly logged into the various job searching sites she'd been using to see if anything new was being advertised which might suit her. There wasn't. She suspected she'd have to start spreading her net even wider very soon.

She had to get out of her flat and have a change of scenery. She decided to go for a walk and fill in some time by going to the supermarket, wandering around her local Tesco like a zombie, not really sure what she was putting in her trolley and checking her phone every minute or so. She made it to the checkout and paid. How long had John had to wait before the ambulance arrived, she wondered. What hospital would he be taken to? Had anyone examined him? Maybe she should call the hospitals local to the farm? Would she be told anything though? She longed to get in her car and be with Mark to support him, she could only imagine what he must be going through, but he'd made it obvious that he didn't want her there.

With all these thoughts whirling around her mind, Polly found herself back at the door to her flat. She let herself in and was dumping her bags of food on the side in the kitchen ready to unpack when she heard a ding from her mobile. She pulled it out of her pocket, dropping it on the floor and cursing herself for her clumsiness in her haste. Picking it up again, she saw she had a text message from Maggie: "Hello love, Mark asked me to message you. I'm at the hospital with John and he's doing much better. They're going to keep him in overnight for observation. He didn't have a heart attack, the doctors think it's angina. He needs to take it easy for a bit, but he's going to be fine."

Polly hurriedly wrote a thank you message to Maggie and sent it before bursting into tears. She was so, so grateful that John was going to be alright, but so upset that her actions had blown up so spectacularly and caused him to be unwell. Not only that she was heartbroken that the friendship and trust between them was destroyed. She wished she'd had the opportunity to explain herself properly but Polly doubted she'd ever have a chance to now.

* * *

Polly woke up the next morning still feeling wretched. She couldn't get the look on Mark's face as he called for the ambulance out of her mind. She needed to do something positive. Her first thought was to message Maggie and ask what hospital John was in so she could see him, but she quickly realised how selfish that would be: she'd be putting Maggie in a very awkward situation if Mark and John didn't want her to visit. And if Maggie did tell her where John was, how would she feel if John had a setback because he got upset when she turned up? Plus, Aunt Sue would probably be there. This last thought put a final nail in the coffin of her idea. She couldn't face another showdown with that horrible woman. How could Sue live with herself after what she'd done? Well, she'd provided all the evidence of Sue's misdemeanours, now wasn't the time to go through them again, and the documentation was still at the farmhouse for John and Mark to look at if they chose to. She could do no more.

Turning her thoughts from John, Polly pondered how she'd managed to get herself into this mess in the first place. Why couldn't she have just been honest with her parents and her sister about losing her job? Had she really let her pride get the better of her like this? How had her relationship with them all deteriorated to this point? They'd always been close.

Polly knew she needed to speak to her family in person, it wasn't something to do over the phone, wimping out of conversing with them properly as she so often did now. There was no time like the present — well, after lunch anyway. Her mum and dad's house was slightly closer than her sister's, and so Polly convinced herself that it made sense for her to visit them first. She knew enough of their schedule to be pretty certain she'd find them at home.

Pulling into their driveway a couple of hours later, she spotted Julie's people carrier parked next to her mum's little blue Ford Fiesta. This was not unusual, she knew Julie spent a lot of time at their parents', but facing everyone at once had not been the plan. If she hadn't been worried she'd been spotted arriving by someone glancing through the window, she probably would have turned around and left, but it was time to face the music.

Her mum, Ruth, was at the front door by the time Polly was getting out of her car.

"Well, this is a lovely surprise!" Ruth said warmly. "Julie's here as well, she popped by for a cup of tea before picking up Michael. Have you got a day off work?"

"That's actually what I've come to talk to you about," Polly explained, giving her a hug.

They walked into the kitchen where Julie and her dad were having a cup of tea together. They greeted her with equal astonishment.

"Would you like a drink and a custard cream?" her mother asked. "The kettle just boiled."

"Sure, that would be nice," Polly replied.

"Why aren't you at work?" Julie asked in her usual blunt manner.

"I lost my job," Polly said bluntly. She'd planned to do more of a lead-up and break the news to her parents gently, but at least it was out of the way now. Everyone stared at her.

"What?" said her mother and father simultaneously.

"Why?" asked Julie.

Polly sat down at the end of the kitchen table, the place that had always been hers when she was growing up. She'd spent so many hours at that table, eating meals, painting, doing homework . . . she fiddled with a small, smooth lump on the tabletop. She seemed to recall it being made by a splodge of modelling glue she hadn't cleaned up quickly enough.

"I was made redundant," she explained. "Basically, they were cutting back within the company to make it more efficient, just like they cut back in all the businesses they helped recover. I was 'expendable' apparently."

"Oh no!" said her mum, rushing over to put her arms around Polly.

"Did they give you a decent redundancy package?" Julie demanded.

"No, I was there for less than two years so, according to my contract, they didn't have to pay me a penny."

"Typical," said her dad. "But you'll be back on your feet in no time, love. A clever girl like you'll be snapped up for an even better job straight away."

Polly couldn't help noticing a flash of something pass over her sister's face. What was it? Anger? Resentment? Polly wasn't sure, but she put it to the back of her mind as she said, "I wish that were the case — but I was actually made redundant in January. I've been looking for a job ever since, but haven't had any luck."

"How have you been managing for money?" asked her dad gently, his brow creased with worry.

"I've been doing shifts in a local pub. It doesn't pay fantastically, but it's kept the wolves from the door." Polly hung her head, embarrassed.

"Well, this has come as quite a shock," Polly's dad said. "And I'm sorry you felt you couldn't confide in us all sooner, we'd always want to support you if you're having a rough time of things."

"I know."

"It can't have been easy to move from what you were doing to working behind a bar, but you needed the money and you knuckled down. I don't like to think how many hours a week you must be working to afford the rent on that flat of yours."

"Thanks, Dad," Polly said. Now, with hindsight, she didn't really know why she'd been so reluctant to tell them, she already felt so much lighter.

"So that's how come you had so much time to spend at that farm," said Julie.

"Yes. They're paying me a commission, but aside from that, it was so good to be contributing to something I really believed in, and watching it turn itself around was really rewarding."

"All thanks to my girl's ideas," said her dad proudly.

"Not all!" said Polly, laughing.

"Are you going to do more work for them?" asked her mum.

"No, no, that's all finished now," Polly said. "I had an interview the other day for a marketing company that went well," she continued, changing the subject.

"That's great," said her dad.

"Never feel like you have to hide anything from us, darling," said her mum reaching for her hand.

"I know, Mum. I'm sorry. I didn't think I would be out of work for long and then I could just tell you I had a new job. But the more time went by, the bigger the lie became."

"But why lie to us in the first place?" her dad persisted.

"I guess I didn't want to disappoint you. You were so proud of me, and I made such a big deal about my job."

"We're still proud of you, sweetheart. You've supported yourself for months with the work you could find. That's impressive. You must tell us if you need any help, financially, or anything," said her dad. "We're always here for you."

"Oh Julie, look," said Ruth, pointing to the clock on the oven. "It's time for you to get Michael."

"Can I come with you?" Polly found herself asking. She could sense that something was up with her sister and she needed to get to the bottom of it.

"Erm . . . sure," said Julie, looking surprised.

Polly said a quick goodbye to her parents, promising to be back soon for a longer chat, Julie would drop her back there after picking up Michael.

Polly followed her sister to her car and got in the passenger seat. Julie had reversed out of the driveway and was half a mile down the road when Polly could bear it no more and broke the silence. "Julie, what's up? You seem upset about something."

"Me? Nothing. What have I got to be upset about?" Julie's green eyes flashed and her hands were rigid on the steering wheel.

"I don't know," said Polly, calmly. "But you're not yourself. Are you angry with me for not telling you about losing my job?"

"No," said Julie, her shoulders relaxing a little. "I get why you didn't, and I don't blame you. I'd probably do the same thing if I was Mum and Dad's golden girl. Wouldn't want to disappoint them," she muttered.

"You think I'm their golden girl?" repeated Polly, incredulously.

"Are you kidding me? Of course you are! Did you hear Dad — 'A clever girl like you'? I've been looking for a part-time job for months and you know what he said to me, 'Why? You're better off with the kids'!"

"I'm sure he didn't mean it badly," Polly said, quickly. "He just knows how much you like spending time with them, and what a great mum you are."

Julie snorted. "Yeah, right."

"I honestly think that's all it was. How come you're looking for a job anyway? Is everything alright with Phil?"

"Yeah, Phil's job is great, but with Michael starting school full-time in September, there's not much for me to do all day. The house only needs so much cleaning, and it gets kind of . . . lonely."

"You never said," Polly replied, surprised at her sister's revelation that her seemingly perfect life wasn't quite all it seemed.

"You never asked," Julie shot back, before sighing. "I love my kids and I love my husband, but I need something to do during the day. And I haven't been able to find anything — no one wants to employ a mother with nothing on her CV since she got married eight years ago."

"Hey, it's not just you. I can't find a job either," Polly reminded her.

"You have a point there . . ." said Julie with a smile.

"Why didn't you talk to me about this before?"

"I thought you'd think I was being daft, wanting a job when I don't have to work and making such a fuss about not being able to get one. It's only a part-time job after all, even sixteen-year-olds manage to get them!"

"What sort of thing did you want to do?"

"I don't know. I think that's part of the problem. Some of my mum friends have set up businesses, but you know me, I can't do crafts and the fairy cakes I make with the kids are hardly *Bake Off* worthy. And it needs to be flexible because I can only work during school hours, and only really during term time."

"Maybe there's something you could do from home?" suggested Polly. "You're really organised: you could be one of those virtual assistants!"

"Thanks for the suggestion, Pol, you're sweet. And thanks for listening. I'm sorry I was all weird."

"Don't worry, and I'm sure you'll find something soon."

"You will too, and it'll be so much better than your last place."

"Thanks, Julie." They pulled up outside the little village school the children went to. "Is that Michael in the playground?"

"Yep," Julie said, waving to her son. "He's going to be so excited to have his auntie coming to pick him up. Why don't we take him for a milkshake?"

"That's a great idea," said Polly, happily. Everything else in her life may have gone to pot, but my goodness, it felt good to be on better terms with Julie: who would have thought they'd both have the same problem, but neither had felt able to tell the other?

* * *

It was harder for Polly to hold on to her happy mood when she was back home and by herself later that day. Everything seemed to remind her of Mark — from her mud-encrusted wellington boots by her front door to the empty mug shoved underneath the sofa because she still hadn't got round to buying a coffee table.

She wished she could just forget about him and move on — she was so desperate to that she was close to agreeing to another one of Alice's blind date set-ups.

Despite their inauspicious start, she'd been so sure that Mark was a good guy, someone she could trust. He was kind to his father, and so patient and caring towards the animals on the farm. But the fact that he didn't think to confide in her had her questioning her judgement again.

Maybe he hadn't realised Polly was interested in him, she had done her best to hide it after all so she could maintain at least a hint of professionalism. Or possibly he'd been stringing her along — knowing she liked him and enjoying the attention. Though as much as she wanted to hate Mark, she couldn't believe that to be true, and there'd been times when she had been sure her desire for him had been reciprocated but not acted on, she'd assumed because of them working together.

It could just be that the topic of his girlfriend never came up, Polly guessed, but it seemed unlikely. It was frustrating to think she'd probably never know the truth. She was left with the feeling of excruciating embarrassment and a wish that things could have been different between them.

CHAPTER FOURTEEN

Two days later, Polly received a phone call with an offer for the job she'd interviewed for the day before John was taken ill. She had absolutely no regrets after she immediately politely declined it. She wasn't going to settle for a good-enough career anymore.

Working on Nightingale Farm and seeing its fortunes turn around had made Polly happy, far happier than her previous, much higher paid job had. She'd felt she was making a difference and she wanted to do that every day. She could manage financially working at the Bluebell for a while longer until she found something right for her, not just a job that paid the bills. Could she set up her own business? Maybe even move in with her parents again until it was bringing in enough money to support her? There must be a way for her to recapture at least some of the joy that Nightingale Farm brought her, and for her to have more control over her future.

Her door buzzer rang and she absentmindedly answered it, her mind teeming with ideas — none of which were quite right yet, but she hoped she'd get there.

Polly's stomach somersaulted when she heard Mark's voice on the other end of the intercom.

"Hi," he said. "Can I come up for a few minutes?"

"Um . . . Sure," Polly replied. What else could she say? She cursed herself for being dressed in old yoga pants and a t-shirt at least two sizes too big for her. At least she'd washed her hair that morning.

A moment later, Mark was at her flat door, carrying a beautiful pine coffee table.

"I promised you a table," Mark said gruffly. He marched past her and continued into the sitting room, placing his gift down in front of the sofa.

"Thank you, it's beautiful," Polly said automatically. She was so confused by this bizarre situation, that she didn't really know what she was saying.

Mark shrugged. He shifted uncomfortably from foot to foot.

"I didn't expect you to give me anything after everything that's happened . . ."

"I want you to have it."

Polly nodded. "How's your dad?"

She unconsciously held her breath until he replied, "Much better. He's home now."

"I'm so glad." Polly waited for Mark to say something else. She sensed he wanted to, but he was silent.

"Would you like a drink?" she finally asked, perplexed, but wanting to do something to make Mark stay.

"A tea would be great."

"Why don't you make yourself comfortable and I'll bring it through in a minute," Polly suggested, feeling a bit like a waitress, but wanting to avoid the awkward standing around together waiting for the kettle to boil.

"Okay," replied Mark.

When Polly rejoined him a couple of minutes later, Mark was examining her bookshelf. He turned as she came in and gave her a clumsy smile.

She put the drinks on coasters on the coffee table, doing her best not to catch his eye.

"I hope you don't mind me dropping in like this," he said, rubbing the back of his neck with his hand. "I needed to speak to you in person about what happened."

"Of course, I don't. It's lovely to see you. I've been feeling so bad about your dad . . ."

"Please don't," Mark said quickly. "As soon as I got back from the hospital the day Dad was taken ill, I went through the papers you'd left on the kitchen table. It was already late when I started, but I looked at everything. What you'd said about Aunt Sue was completely right, all the evidence was there. I wanted to call you straight away, but it was about three in the morning and I needed to speak to Dad about it first. Sorry . . . I'm rambling." He stopped and took a breath. "I couldn't speak to Dad until he was completely out of danger because I knew it would upset him again."

"I can understand that." Polly wrapped her arms around herself at the memory of John collapsed on the floor.

"I felt so terrible about what had happened, I wanted to tell you face-to-face. Now Dad's out of hospital, we've spoken through everything. Maggie's been staying to look after him so it was fine for me to drive up here."

"She's in the spare bedroom I imagine?" Polly couldn't help asking with a tentative smile.

"Supposedly." Mark grinned. "But you know how squeaky those hall floorboards are."

It felt so good to be sharing a joke together.

"Dad wanted to come too," Mark continued. "He didn't believe what Sue was saying for a moment, he kept saying so in the hospital, but I wanted him to calm down, he was getting so worked up."

"You sent me away," Polly said bluntly, the hurt of her last encounter with Mark coming flooding back.

"Because I needed to focus on Dad and getting him to the hospital."

"You didn't send Sue away."

"No," admitted Mark. "But she's my aunt and Dad's sister. I didn't feel it was my place."

Polly nodded. She understood, but that didn't make it any easier to swallow.

"Plus, did you really want to be facing off with Aunt Sue in the farmyard when the ambulance arrived?"

Polly couldn't help smiling at the image. "No," she admitted.

"As soon as I was convinced Dad was out of danger, I took him through all the figures you'd left on the table, along with your notes. He agreed it was obvious who was behind the discrepancies in the farm accounts."

"How did he take it?"

"Honestly? He was really upset, mostly about how you'd been treated. He was hurt by Sue's actions, but it was the fact he hadn't told you he believed you straight away which he feels terrible about."

"I don't blame him for that at all," said Polly, quickly. "I was accusing his sister of something horrible and didn't have a chance to show him any of the evidence I'd collected. But I made sure I was absolutely certain, I swear."

"I know you did, and the evidence was clear as day once a light had been thrown on it."

Mark was being lovely, and it was wonderful to hear that he and John believed her, but Polly knew she had to address the other elephant in the room. "About what Sue said . . . about me losing my job . . ." she began.

Mark put up his hand to stop her. "That's your business," he said simply. Seeing the uncertainty on Polly's face, he continued, "We didn't hire you because you had a fancy career. In fact, I was worried you wouldn't be able to devote enough time to us with you having a full-time job. It was your ideas which made us trust you with our home and our business."

"Yes . . ." Polly said, "but I lied to you."

"I wish you hadn't felt the need to do that," Mark admitted.

"So do I. As time went on it seemed to get harder and harder to extract myself from it."

Mark nodded. "Lies tend to do that."

"It was much easier just not to tell my family what had happened — I never imagined I'd need to lie to anyone else as well."

"Well, families can be complicated things."

"Yes, they can," Polly said, her head down. "I really did feel dreadful not confiding the truth about my job to your dad," she admitted.

"He understands why you did it. He doesn't hold it against you."

"That's very good of him."

"He's a good guy."

"He is," said Polly. "And what about you?" she asked, her heart in her mouth. "Can you forgive me for lying to you?"

"Yes," said Mark firmly. "I can't say I wish you hadn't done it, and that I wasn't hurt when I found out, but I guess I understand, and I can't entirely blame you. I didn't exactly make it easy for you when you first came to help us."

A little smile couldn't help forming on Polly's lips as she recalled how grumpy Mark had been to her when she first met him.

"I didn't think you had any idea what you were doing," explained Mark. "You were a city girl who didn't look like she'd ever set foot in a farmyard before. I thought you'd charge us a fortune for a bunch of kooky ideas which would end up getting us further into debt."

"And did I prove you wrong?" challenged Polly, gently. Through it all, the one thing she was proud of was how her suggestions had helped the farm. She knew there was no denying that.

"You proved me very wrong, in a lot of ways," Mark replied, his cheeks reddening in a very endearing way.

"Thank you for coming here to tell me. I appreciate it. Would it be alright for me to visit your dad soon?"

"Of course, he'd absolutely love that."

They stood facing each other awkwardly. Polly thought Mark was going to leave but it seemed there was more he needed to say.

"So, how have you been?" he asked finally.

"Not too bad, thanks," Polly said. "I've been spending more time with my niece and nephew which has been lovely. I had a bit of a heart to heart with my family, and we sorted a lot of stuff out."

"That's good to hear."

"It was a long time coming," Polly admitted.

"How are things on the work front?"

"I've been doing any shifts I can at the local pub. It's not ideal, but it's not forever. I was actually offered a job . . ."

Mark's face fell.

". . . but I decided not to accept it, it wasn't right for me."

"Oh, good," Mark blurted out.

Polly's eyebrows rose in surprise, and Mark, worried he'd offended her, swiftly continued, "It's just that I have a proposition for you."

Polly's eyebrows rose even further.

"Obviously we can't use Aunt Sue to do our accounts now, but with my carpentry taking off and Dad needing to rest up more, there's quite a bit to do. I'd like Dad to be able to focus on his market garden and have the money side of things taken care of. We wouldn't be able to pay you as much as the jobs you're applying for, I'm sure, but there's another cottage on our land which we're renovating which is yours if you'd like it so accommodation is included . . ."

"You're offering me a job?" asked Polly, incredulously, hardly daring to believe it.

"Yes!" Mark said, running his hand through his dark hair — he obviously wasn't finding this easy. "We'd like you to be a sort of farm manager — organising any projects still on the go, or waiting to be started, overseeing the bookings for the cottages, dealing with marketing and social media . . ."

"Would that include bottle feeding new-born lambs in the middle of the night?"

"Possibly," admitted Mark. "I'll have to add that to the job description. If you'd like to, we'd love you to start as soon as possible."

Polly's heart leapt — Mark's offer was a dream come true — yes, she'd be earning much less than she would if she were to get a job in London, but she wouldn't have nearly as many outgoings, and she'd be happy doing a job she enjoyed. She'd even be living on the farm surrounded by those beautiful views, and neighbour to John and Mark.

Her thoughts were abruptly brought up short: wait, what was she thinking even contemplating Mark's offer? She couldn't possibly work alongside him every day, living so close to him, when she felt the way she did about him. How would she manage seeing him and Sophia together? What if Sophia moved into the farmhouse? What if they had children, and she had to watch their perfect family living their perfect life every day, the life she so longed for with Mark, while she existed in a poor imitation of it in a little cottage on the other side of the farm?

"That's such a wonderful offer . . ." she began, knowing that as much as she might want to accept now, it wouldn't be the right thing for her. Not if she couldn't be with Mark.

Panic flashed across Mark's face as he realised she was about to refuse him, making Polly stop in bewilderment: she knew he felt bad about not believing her revelation about Aunt Sue earlier, but it wouldn't be that difficult for him to find someone else to take on the farm manager job surely? Why did he look so worried?

"Before you say what I think you're about to say," Mark said quickly, "There's something else I need to tell you . . ."

"Okay . . ." Polly said.

"Right, well, the thing is . . ." he continued hesitantly. "The thing is . . ."

He seemed incapable of meeting her eye and looked so troubled, Polly blurted out, "Your dad is alright, isn't he? There's nothing you're not telling me?"

"No, no! It's nothing like that!" Mark immediately replied. "It's . . . oh, I'm just going to say it . . . I have feelings for you."

Polly froze. "What?"

"That wasn't quite the reaction I was hoping for."

"You have feelings for me?" clarified Polly, disbelievingly.

"Yes. I have for quite a while actually."

"Feeling feelings?" Polly clarified.

"Yes, Dad's cider seemed to decide it for me." He gave a wry smile.

Polly's head was swimming as she tried to take in what Mark was saying. "But you pushed me away and ignored me the next day," she protested. "I mean, the day after the night we drank the cider," she managed to say.

"You ignored me too!" Mark replied. "In fact, you ran away. And I only stopped kissing you because I didn't want to take advantage."

"I thought you were drunk and regretted kissing me."

"I thought the same about you."

Polly put her head in her hands, there was just so much to take in. Mark cautiously came over to her. His gaze softened as it met hers and he took her hand.

"I tried to get you out of my mind," he explained. "The farm was beginning to come together and I didn't want to jeopardise that by making a fool of myself with you. But then we started to spend more time together, and I managed to relax more and not be quite so grumpy and stressed around you. I appreciated you supporting me in setting my carpentry business back up again and we were getting along really well. I wanted to tell you about my feelings the night I stayed over at your flat, but I chickened out. I made up the breakfast meeting I told you I had because I didn't think I'd be able to see you and not tell you how I felt.

"Anyway," he said with a sigh. "I had to say something now because if you're not going to be our farm manager, I might not get another chance to."

"What about your girlfriend?" Polly asked, suddenly remembering Sophia.

"I don't have a girlfriend," Mark replied immediately, looking bemused.

"But Aunt Sue said you were seeing her goddaughter, Sophia . . ." Polly said, quietly, realising as soon as the words were out of her mouth how stupid she'd been to believe anything Aunt Sue had told her. "She was lying, wasn't she?"

Mark rolled his eyes. "She's been trying to set me up with Sophia for years, but she's not my type and I'm not hers. We're friends though. She came round for supper a while ago because she was interested in commissioning a piece from me . . ." he paused. "That was the day you were supposed to be staying for supper, wasn't it? But you told Dad you had to leave early because of work?"

"That's right," Polly said, cringing at the memory.

"So, there was no work problem?"

"No," Polly admitted. "Aunt Sue told me you and Sophia were together, and that Sophia would be joining us for supper."

"And you scarpered?"

"Pretty much."

"Because of Sophia?" Mark clarified.

"Yes, because of Sophia."

"I thought I'd come across too strong and you were staying away because you weren't interested in me. I was worried I'd made you feel awkward."

"No, not at all!"

Mark's face broke into a broad grin. "Is it safe for me to assume that means you might have feelings for me too?"

"Yes," Polly said, lifting her head to meet his gaze. "I think that cider had the same effect on me as it did on you."

Mark pulled her into his arms, and almost before Polly knew what was happening, they were kissing fiercely. "Finally," her body seemed to call out as she sank into his.

When they eventually pulled apart, Mark whispered, "I love you."

"That escalated fast," said Polly, her heart beating so fast it threatened to burst out of her chest.

Mark gazed anxiously into her eyes. "I didn't want to freak you out. Are you freaked out?"

"I'm not freaked out," Polly reassured him. "I think I love you too."

"So, have I convinced you to accept my job offer?"

"Absolutely," Polly laughed. "You should have given more details initially, I didn't realise how many perks were included before. How soon can I start?"

EPILOGUE

The big day dawned crisp and bright. Having a wedding on a farm in mid-October was definitely taking a chance, and had created a very busy couple of months of planning and organising, but everyone involved had agreed with the bride and groom that there was no point in them waiting. They were traditional enough to want to be married before they shared a home and began their life together, but weren't prepared to hang on a day longer than they had to. They wanted their married life to start as soon as possible.

Thankfully a spell of dry weather meant the marquee for the ceremony was able to be erected in a field behind the farmhouse as planned, with the huge flourishing pumpkin patch in the background.

The small reception was to be held in the café, which looked beautiful festooned with pale-blue bunting and balloons. The wedding cake sat on the counter alongside the champagne flutes ready for everyone to toast the happy couple.

As the ceremony began, John's nerves were apparent as he kept his gaze fixed on the tent's opening, but Polly knew Mark and Dylan would keep him calm.

A huge smile, matching his bride's, broke across John's face as Maggie appeared at the entrance to the marquee.

She looked beautiful in a chic ivory shift dress and jacket. Happiness radiated from her as she began walking confidently towards her husband-to-be.

John had been so worried about how Mark would react when he admitted his feelings for Maggie, but his news was hardly a revelation to Mark, and he was glad his father had found happiness again.

Polly, thrilled to be bridesmaid, followed Maggie down the aisle. She smiled at her niece and nephew sitting between Julie and Phil. They were already beginning to fidget — the highlight of the day for them would be when they got to change out of their smart clothes and into the overalls and wellies they kept at their Aunt Polly's house.

Julie looked so much happier now she was working as the events planner for the farm, her latest sell-out event was a pumpkin carving party in a couple of weeks' time. Polly's mum and dad were alongside her sister's family. Polly had been very touched when John and Maggie had invited all her family to their special day, it showed how much she meant to them and how they were including her in their life.

Maggie made it to the top of the aisle and took her place beside John and Dylan, who sat, dignified next to his master, his usual bounciness curtailed. He seemed to understand the gravity of the situation, and the importance of his role in it. He was the ring bearer after all.

Polly's eyes locked with Mark's and they smiled at each other. He looked ridiculously handsome in his morning suit, his hair slightly shorter than usual as he'd had a trim to tidy it up the week before. The frown of worry, which had seemed a permanent fixture when they'd first met, no longer sat firmly on his brow. The farm was turning a good profit finally, and his own carpentry business was doing better than it ever had in Brighton.

Polly moved to the side and took in the whole scene in front of her; all the people she loved most in the world gathered together in her favourite place. How her life had changed in less than a year, she wouldn't wish for it to be any other way.

* * *

It was hours later before Polly and Mark managed to slip away for a few minutes of quiet together. The day had gone brilliantly, and Polly felt a huge sense of relief after the weeks of planning and weather watching.

Mark carried a blanket, a bottle of champagne and two glasses and led her up a track to the highest point of the remaining farmland from which they could look down on the farmyard and see the guests milling around with Dylan keeping everyone in order.

Mark laid the blanket down on the grass and poured them both a drink. They sat close together for warmth, grateful for the coats they'd pulled on over their wedding outfits.

"Won't we be missed?" Polly asked, anxiously.

"They'll be alright without us for a while," replied Mark.

Contentment flowed through Polly as she watched the scene below.

"A lot's changed since you showed up, leaving gates open all over the place and forcing me to buy fancy organic soaps," said Mark, wrapping his arms around her, an action so familiar now, but which still gave Polly a little extra buzz of happiness.

"It certainly has," Polly replied, tilting her face up for a kiss.

She felt Mark give a deep sigh of satisfaction. He was a very different man from the grouchy ogre she'd met when she first visited Nightingale Farm. He was content, proud of his work, and excited about the future. The knowledge that at least a small part of that transformation was thanks to her meant Polly was now absolutely certain she was exactly where she should be.

Polly's happy musings were interrupted by Mark pointing to the farmhouse. "Bloody roof tiles still need replacing."

"We'll get to it," said Polly, squeezing his hand.

"I know."

Mark rubbed the back of his neck, and moved his body away from Polly's, fiddling in his coat pockets. "I actually had an ulterior motive for getting you up here . . ." he said, slowly. "The last few months with you, Pol . . . they've been amazing — the change in the farm, the change in my whole life, it's down to you."

"I don't think . . ." Polly interrupted, but Mark placed a finger gently on her mouth.

"Let me finish," he said, gently. "You know I'm not great with words, and I really want to do this right."

Polly nodded, watching him.

"You make everything better," Mark continued. "You make me better." He took a deep breath. "I want to spend the rest of my life with you, here, on the farm. To keep building the business together. To raise a family together."

Polly's eyes shone as she struggled to hold back tears of joy.

"Would you do me the honour of agreeing to be my wife?" Mark asked. Polly shook with nerves and excitement as she opened the small, black box he handed her. A delicate white gold solitaire diamond ring was nestled inside.

"It was my mum's engagement ring, Dad and I thought she'd like you to have it, but if you'd prefer something different . . ."

"It's perfect," Polly whispered.

"Please say yes," he whispered back.

"Yes," said Polly, smiling up at him. "Absolutely, yes."

THE END

ALSO BY EMMA BENNET

HER PERFECT HERO
THE GREEN HILLS OF HOME
THE ONE THAT GOT AWAY?
STARSTRUCK
FALLING IN LOVE AT NIGHTINGALE FARM

The Joffe Books Story

We began in 2014 when Jasper agreed to publish his mum's much-rejected romance novel and it became a bestseller.

Since then we've grown into the largest independent publisher in the UK. We're extremely proud to publish some of the very best writers in the world, including Joy Ellis, Faith Martin, Caro Ramsay, Helen Forrester, Simon Brett and Robert Goddard. Everyone at Joffe Books loves reading and we never forget that it all begins with the magic of an author telling a story.

We are proud to publish talented first-time authors, as well as established writers whose books we love introducing to a new generation of readers.

We have been shortlisted for Independent Publisher of the Year at the British Book Awards three times, in 2020, 2021 and 2022, and for the Diversity and Inclusivity Award at the Independent Publishing Awards in 2022.

We built this company with your help, and we love to hear from you, so please email us about absolutely anything bookish at:

feedback@joffebooks.com

If you want to receive free books every Friday and hear about all our new releases, join our mailing list here:

www.joffebooks.com/contact

And when you tell your friends about us, just remember: it's pronounced Joffe as in coffee or toffee!

www.ingramcontent.com/pod-product-compliance
Lightning Source LLC
Chambersburg PA
CBHW021958190626
46808CB00017B/2452